THE REGENT'S KNIGHT

THE REGENT'S KNIGHT

BY J.M. SNYDER

jms books

THE REGENT'S KNIGHT

JMS Books LLC
10286 Staples Mill Rd. #221
Glen Allen, VA 23060
www.jms-books.com

Printed in the United States of America

ISBN: 9781-4-6363-017-1

CHAPTER 1

PRINCE AMERY LLEWELLEN, heir to the throne of Pharr, heard the fanfare as each of his knights arrived at the castle. But he waited for the knock on his chamber door before rousing himself from his pensive stance by the fire. "Come in," he said, turning as his young page entered. "Well?"

"They're here, Your Highness." The boy bowed low before the regent, his long blond-white ponytail sliding over one shoulder. His hair paled against the blue and silver cloak he wore that matched Amery's ornate coverlet.

Amery frowned to belay the sudden excitement coursing through his veins. His old friends had responded to his summons, as he had expected. As he'd *hoped*. "All of them?"

Of course, all of them, he chided silently. He'd counted four separate trumpets before the sun set, had he not?

Still, the boy nodded in confirmation. "Yes, Your Highness," he said. "Sir Giles from the westlands, Sir Berik from the north, Sir Lohden—"

"And Sir Tovin?"

Watch it, Amery warned himself. *No one's to know, and you'll damage all the two of you have carefully built over the years just because you're too eager to see him again. You know the servants talk. You've heard the whispered rumors when they think you don't hear. You don't need to confirm that gossip.*

Scowling to cover his emotions, Amery glared at the page and spat, "I'm sure *he's* here, as well."

"He is," the boy confirmed. Glancing up at the regent, he frowned slightly, as if he bore bad news, then in a rush, he whispered, "They're in the drawing room, Your Highness. The maids fear there will be words between you and Sir Tovin again, like last time."

Amery grinned. *Last time*...how long had it been since he'd seen the knight from the southland? A few months, easily. The last time, Tovin Raimus had come to the castle under the pretense of defense plans for the southern border, but he and Amery had spent more time hidden in the bedroom than the war room. *Only the servants don't know that.* All the chambermaids had heard were angry shouts and loud arguments that rang through the halls, a scuffle here, a fistfight there, anything to keep them from suspecting that their regent spent his nights in the arms of his favorite knight.

And admit it, Amery told himself, straightening his coverlet. *You like the fights. They turn you on—they turn you BOTH on. It's so much sweeter when you must kiss and make up.*

Everyone in the kingdom knew of the "bad blood" between Prince Amery and Sir Tovin; their fights were legendary, at times ringing through the castle halls and spooking the servants into hiding. The arguments had started early, just after Amery came of an age to assume the throne, and had only grown worse in the years since his father, King Adin, had disappeared among the battles to the north. As long as no one suspected it was all a farce, Amery saw no reason to change the common belief.

"Your Highness?" his page prompted. Amery roused himself from his musing, frowning into the flames that guttered low in the fireplace as he smoothed his hands down the front of his coverlet. "They're waiting."

"Right."

Amery glanced at himself in the battered shield that hung above the fireplace. The shield and the sword displayed beneath it were all that remained of his father; they had been found on the battlefield two years prior, their bearer's body still not recovered. The man of twenty-three summers who Amery saw reflected back in the shield was a mere shadow of the king—he often wondered how long he'd be able to hold off barbaric invaders his father couldn't even control. King Adin had often spoken of putting the populace first, a trick Amery hadn't yet learned. Yes, he loved the castle, with its opulence, its silent halls, its bevy of servants to wait on his every whim. He loved the throne, the position it gave him in others' eyes, the way it straightened his spine. He'd proven himself a fair ruler, just and kind... 'accessible' was how the people referred to him, his advisors said.

But his heart burned for one thing, one *man*, and he'd give up the castle and all its trappings, the throne, the entire land if he had to, if he *could*, just to make Sir Tovin his.

Running a quick hand through his long, smooth hair, as if a strand of the dark red thicket would dare stray out of place, Amery frowned at himself before turning away. *Just have to keep up appearances until tonight*, he thought as he followed the page from his chamber. *Just until I can get Tovin alone again.*

He couldn't wait.

✦

GROWING UP, AMERY had been given free reign throughout the castle. The only son of the King of Pharr, prince in title, and soon to be regent himself, nothing stood in Amery's path. Whenever his tutors released him from his studies, he ran like a wild child through the castle, footsteps ringing off the stone floors, boyish laughter shrill in otherwise quiet corridors. He'd race through the gardens, around the stables, happy to be *free* from the dry books and dusty men his father hired to teach him.

During his tenth year, he grew mischievous and daring, testing the limits of his father's—and the servants'—patience. On the first clear day of spring, the winter air had finally begun to warm up a bit, and nature's siren-like call grew impossible for the young prince to ignore. He'd ventured out into the stables and found a small toad, which he brought back to the castle and tucked into the linens to tease a young chambermaid. As her shrieks chased him from the castle, Amery sprinted into the garden, his mind already wandering to his next trick…

The sound of clashing swords stopped him short.

Beneath an old weathered oak, four boys brandished weapons at each other, swinging short, blunt broadswords in dangerous arcs. They were all equally mismatched—a tall, thin kid fought against a big, brawny guy and, dueling beside them, a sturdy boy twice Amery's height battled a short, squat kid. Their blades flashed in the dappled sunlight as Amery approached, mesmerized. When he came within earshot and they still hadn't noticed him, he called out, "*I* am the Prince of Pharr."

The thin, gawkish boy staggered back beneath the weight of his larger opponent's blade. "So?" he sneered. "Go away. You'll get hurt."

Amery ignored the command. "I'll not. Let me fence with you. I'm Amery. And you are…?"

From the other duo of duelers, the taller boy laughed. Amery found his whole body prickling at the sound, so sudden, so carefree. He wondered what he had said to elicit that laugh, and what he could possibly say to hear it again.

In a deep voice that had already changed to that of a man's, the boy called out, "The prince has asked you a question, Loh. Best answer it before you incur his wrath."

The boy called Loh snorted, derisive. "Yeah."

When he said nothing further, Amery cleared his throat, lest they forget he was there. "Loh, is it? Are you guys knights?"

"Gonna be," Loh's opponent said. Sweat dripped from the boy's dark hair, wetting down the start of a thick beard he already wore despite his young age. "That's Lohden. He's ignorant, don't mind him."

"Am *not*." With the flat of his blade, Lohden slapped his sword against his beefy opponent's arm. "You're the ignorant one, Berik. You'd lie with anything for a moment's pleasure. I heard they found you in the stables this morning…oof!"

Berik's sword came down hard, the face behind it clenched like a fist. "You take that back! I was visiting the stable maid."

Beside them, the handsome boy laughed again. Amery's heart soared to hear him, and without realizing it, he drew nearer to their fight. "Loh's just jealous," the boy said, the tease sharp in his voice. "The horses won't even *look* at him."

"You're next, Tove," Lohden swore. "Once I best this beast…"

Berik's rumbled laughter filled the garden like thunder. Ignoring it, the boy called Tove glanced at Amery over his shoulder. "I apologize for not bowing, Your Highness, but as you can see, you caught us in the midst of battling for our honor."

"Please," Amery said, feeling the heat rise in his cheeks, "just Amery."

Those deep eyes twinkled with mirth. "Well," he said, "'just Amery,' I'm Tovin. My less than worthy opponent is Giles."

"Hey!" The short boy he fenced with bristled as he tried to raise to his full height. Amery snickered—the kid wasn't an inch taller than he himself.

They were teenagers, all four of them, young knights in training. Almost instantly, the prince took a liking to the boys, older than himself and already immortal in his eyes. As they turned back to their swordplay, Amery watched in fascination— the motions their bodies made, the swings of their blades, the deft maneuvering that allowed their swords to dance against each other in a clatter of steel…

Sweat beaded on Tovin's brow; his eyes were narrowed, his teeth bared, as he advanced with quick, hard thrusts that his opponent couldn't parry fast enough. Amery found himself inching closer, holding his breath as he watched the fight between Tovin and Giles. Something inside him screwed up like a bolt in a crossbow, drawn tighter and tighter as he watched the boys, and when the rounded end of Tovin's blade finally glanced off Giles's chest, the young prince whooped in victory. "Yes!"

As he crowed, Giles lunged forward, a scowl on his pug-like face. "Shut it, you!"

Before his blade could touch Amery, Tovin's sword knocked it clear. The tall boy stepped between his friend and the prince. "Giles," he spat. Amery saw his shoulders shake with suppressed rage. "Do you *know* who this is?"

Giles didn't answer. Beside them, Lohden and Berik stopped fighting, drawn to the quiet command in Tovin's low voice. "How *dare* you strike the prince."

"I didn't," Giles started. He looked around, helpless, but at that moment, Lohden and Berik seemed to find the grass and the sky much more interesting and refused to meet his gaze. Turning to Tovin, he tried to explain, "I was just kidding. This sword wouldn't cut a loaf of bread, Tove. You know that. I wouldn't—"

"Then don't," Tovin snapped.

One hand reached around behind his back, feeling for Amery. Without thinking, the prince caught Tovin's hand and gave the fingers a tight, reassuring squeeze before letting go. There was a promise in that touch, a vow of protection that Amery intuitively understood. In that instant, they became friends.

Years later, when that friendship deepened into something more, something Amery had to hide from his father and the rest of the kingdom, he would be able to trace his feelings for Tovin to that moment in time. The love that smothered him from the inside, that made it difficult to breathe in the knight's presence, that made him cry out with lust and passion and *need* whenever they coupled, everything he loved about the man, everything he wanted in him, from him, and more—all those emotions led back through their shared experiences, their shared lives, to coalesce in that one single touch.

✦

AT THE HANDS of those young knights, Amery learned more than all his royal tutors ever managed to instill in their years of training him to ascend the throne. Lohden Krale, a gangly boy with short blonde hair and a braying laugh, was the youngest of the group, but still two years Amery's senior. Tovin was next, thirteen when Amery met him. Then came Berik Brohm, a year older, bear-like, with a roving eye for anything that moved— man, woman, or beast, to hear Lohden tell it. At sixteen, Giles Shanely was the oldest, but the runt of the bunch, and always the first to tease Amery. Time and again, his thinly veiled threats were parried aside by Tovin.

Tovin.

The broad shoulders that looked menacing on Berik were strong and sure on Tovin. His smooth, muscled chest tapered into a narrow waist above slim, lean hips. He had a head full of unruly corkscrews the color of river sand and deep eyes like sapphires. Whenever he looked at Amery, those eyes seemed to light up from within, and a slow, easy smile would spread across his handsome face, igniting a spark deep in the young prince's heart.

Every touch from Tovin, every smile, every wink helped fan the flame set deep within the regent that first day they met. He'd gladly weather a hundred of Lohden's stupid laughs, or any number of Giles's barbed comments, if only for a chance to see Tovin's smile or hear his voice again. Without even realizing it, he'd fallen in love.

CHAPTER 2

THIRTEEN YEARS LATER, little had changed among the friends.

"Touché!"

Sir Tovin's triumphant cry echoed off the stone walls of the drawing room as he brought his sword down on Sir Berik's exposed neck. Commanding troops in the southland gave him little opportunity to gather with his old friends; to pass the time waiting for the regent, they'd decided to spar, to test each other's mettle and see who *really* was the best knight of the kingdom. It was a familiar jest between them, a title Tovin secretly knew belonged to him, if the way he could make the regent beg for his touch in bed had any say in the matter.

The first round of the swordfight was Tovin and Berik; after a playful display, Tovin brought Berik to his knees under a barrage of quick, cutting blows. Now he stood over his friend and resisted the urge to rub in his victory. "I win. Next."

"No fair," Berik said, pushing the sword away. "Best of three, what do you say?"

Sir Giles slapped the back of Berik's bushy head as he

stepped onto the plush carpet they had dubbed the sparring field. The fact that Berik knelt was the only reason Giles could reach. "I say move your fat ass," he snapped as he took an opening stance in front of Tovin. Raising his sword in a challenge, he added, "It's my turn."

Berik sighed and hauled himself to his feet. "Your ass is getting pretty chunky, too," he said, tapping his sword against Giles's backside.

Giles turned to swing at him, but Berik laughed and danced out of reach of his friend's sword. "You would look," Giles growled.

"I would," Berik conceded. His conquests in the bedroom far outnumbered his triumphs on the battlefield, as he was the first to admit. Moving to the sidelines, he stood beside Sir Lohden, who was busy ignoring the whole lot of them, an open book in one hand that he tried desperately to concentrate on while the others sparred. Berik leaned over his friend's shoulder and whispered loudly, "Now *you* have a nice ass, Lohden."

"Shut up," Lohden told him. When Berik took a step closer, he added, "Touch my ass and die by my blade, knight."

With a bored sigh, Tovin leaned on his sword. He'd hoped to beat all three of them before Amery made an appearance. "Are you guys quite through?"

"Quite," Giles agreed. Leveling his sword at Tovin, he grinned. "*En garde!*"

Without further warning, he attacked. Tovin managed to get his own sword up between them and he parried the first thrust, but Giles came at him fast, using his small stature to his advantage. For a few breathless moments Tovin thought he would fall beneath the blade, and he gave ground until the carpet disappeared and the heels of his heavy boots rang off the stone floor. If he left the carpet completely, he'd have to concede the fight, and Giles was the older knight, more experienced, Tovin would give him that—

He heard the chamber door scrape open and from the corner of his eye saw the regent enter the room. *Amery.* At the sight of his lover, strength flooded his body, a sudden rush of adrenaline that gave him the edge he needed to push Giles back. *I can't lose now. I'll never hear the end of it.* Bad enough to be teased by his fellow knights, but by the regent himself? There'd be no end to the comments Amery would make in the bedroom.

The tide of the battle turned as Giles tried desperately to dodge his blows, but Tovin gave into the heat of the moment and the thought of lying in his lover's arms later as a victor. He could almost feel the regent's hand brush across his brow, twining through his shoulder-length hair, straightening his curls between those long, tapered fingers as they made love. That was all the edge he needed to turn the fight in his favor.

Behind him, Amery called out, "Gentlemen." When no one responded, the regent clapped his hands to get their attention.

Not NOW. Tovin lunged for Giles. *Not when I'm winning.*

The older man stumbled back and, for a second, Tovin thought this was it—he had won again. It was down to just him and Lohden then, and *that* was no contest…but Giles caught himself and parried Tovin's next thrust with a deafening strike that numbed Tovin's wrist when their swords clashed. "Giles," he growled, pushing his friend away.

"Gentlemen, *please,*" Amery called out. Tovin laughed at the frustration in the regent's voice. "We have matters to discuss here—"

"We're in the middle of something," Tovin explained, as if Amery couldn't *see* that. "A few more minutes, Your Highness, and we'll be right with you."

He turned and winked at the regent, who stared at him as if stunned. In a harsh whisper, Amery spat, "How *dare* you defy me."

Then Giles's sword crashed down on his again and Tovin cursed himself for letting that smooth hair and those smoldering eyes distract him from the fight. The regent fumbled for control of the moment. "I said—"

Through clenched teeth, Tovin replied, "We heard what you said." He parried Giles's next thrust more easily and slashed at the older man without mercy. "We're ignoring you."

"Tovin," Berik warned, his low voice a growl beneath the clash of steel. "Ye gods, you two, don't start again."

Stepping between the sparring partners, Amery glared at Tovin. The intensity of his gaze set Tovin's blood on fire, but he crushed the lust that rose within him. We're not alone, he reminded himself, stepping around Amery to attack Giles. *Tonight we can smother each other with sweetness but right now the others are here, they don't know, they CAN'T...* "Get out of my way," he snarled, shoving Amery aside.

"Sir Tovin," Amery started, tugging on his arm to distract him. "I am your regent. You obey *me*—"

Giles brought his sword down on Tovin's arm, hard, the steel biting into the metal armor the knight wore to protect himself. With a grimace, he shrugged Amery off and turned to meet Giles's challenge. "This has gone on long enough," he muttered, raising his sword to strike his friend to the ground. "Won't you *fall* already?"

Giles flashed him an unctuous smile. "I'm tenacious."

"Sir Tovin, *listen* to me." The regent caught Tovin's arm again, stepping into the fray. "I command the both of you to stop this *now!*"

Suddenly Giles's blade slipped beneath Tovin's own, dangerously close to Amery. *Too* close. Reacting on instinct alone, Tovin shoved the regent out of reach. As he did so, Giles's blade danced along his armor and slipped easily between the links in Tovin's chain mail.

Bright pain blossomed beneath Tovin's ribs, forcing him to hitch his breath as he spun away from his opponent. "Gah," he gasped. For a heart-stopping moment he staggered on his feet, his knees buckling beneath him. He pressed a hand to his side, as if he could extinguish the fire flaring through him. *I won't fall. I can't. I was supposed to win.* "Giles..."

Then Amery's arms were around him. Tovin let himself fall into his regent's embrace. "Oh, hell," Amery whispered, hands fluttering over Tovin's own. "Let me see. Tove, let me see the wound. Please…"

Above them, Giles's grin turned sick, as if he'd swallowed something unpleasant. "I'm sorry," he was saying to anyone who'd listen, but Amery pushed him away when he tried to lean closer. "I didn't mean—"

"I *told* you to stop it," the regent admonished. "But, no, you won't listen to *me*. I'm just the regent. It's just *my* damn kingdom."

"Shut up," Tovin breathed. In the safety of his lover's arms, he felt the thrill of the battle drain away, leaving him shaky and unsteady. His side throbbed, but it wasn't a stabbing pain—he didn't think the blade had managed to pierce his skin. Taking a deep breath, he sat up and leaned his head against Amery's shoulder. So warm, this body beside his. So strong, these arms that held him. When he glanced up to see the concern written out on Amery's smooth face, he wanted nothing more than to kiss it away.

But they weren't alone. Remembering the others, Tovin sat up on his own and slapped at Amery's hands. "I'm fine," he mumbled, trying to inspect the broken links in his mail, but with everyone crowding around him, he had no light. "I said, I am *fine*. It's just a scratch. Giles isn't that good with the blade and you guys know it, so get off me, all of you."

"Tovin," Berik started.

But Tovin pushed himself to his feet and wobbled for a second before breaking away from them all. "I'm fine," he repeated.

And he was—there was no blood on his surcoat, so the sword hadn't made it past the armor, right? He didn't think so. Cautiously he stretched his arm and felt the muscle pull along his side. "I demand a rematch," he declared. Frowning at his friends, he added, "That didn't count."

Giles's face broke into a toothy grin. "Like hell it didn't count. I won. You fell by my blade—"

"I was distracted," Tovin told him, glaring at Amery, still on his knees. "The regent—"

Amery surged to his feet. "I forbid it," he said hotly. "I did not send for my best knights just so you could maim and kill each other in my drawing room. No."

Ignoring him, Tovin bent to retrieve his sword, but Amery placed one foot over the blade to force the knight to look up at him. "You can spar later. I have things to say that cannot wait."

"We had to wait for you," Tovin reminded him. With a twist of his wrist, he slipped the blade out from beneath Amery's foot, knocking the regent back. "You can wait for us."

"I won," Giles said again. "So now I spar with Lohden."

But Tovin shook his head. "I demanded a rematch. That means the last one didn't count."

"I want a rematch, too," Berik stated. "That's not fair—"

"Shut up," Tovin and Giles chimed in unison.

When Tovin took a challenging stance in front of his old friend, Amery cleared his throat noisily. "A night in the stocks if you fight again," he announced.

Giles wavered between raising his blade to meet Tovin and listening to the commands of his regent. At that hesitation, Amery pressed his advantage. Looking from face to face, he confronted all four of them. "Am I talking here? Is anyone listening?"

"I'm not fighting," Lohden pointed out. He sank into one of the chairs at the conference table and sighed lustily. "Is this going to take all night? Because I have things to do."

"Like what?" Berik wanted to know as he took a seat across from his friend. "Sleep? What an exciting night life you have."

"Giles?" Tovin cajoled. He raised his sword in anticipation. "Are we fighting here or what?"

Giles glanced at Amery's fiery gaze and shrugged. "I didn't come all this way just to sleep in stocks."

"He's bluffing." Tovin knew the regent too well; as long as Tovin was at the castle, he knew *he* wouldn't be sleeping in the prison. The regent would never allow it. No matter how angry Amery grew with him, Tovin knew he'd sleep in the regent's arms at night, but he couldn't say that out loud. Instead, he deepened his voice and intoned, "I challenge you, Sir Giles. Do you deny or accept?"

"Tovin," Giles warned with a jerk of his head in Amery's direction. "Can't this wait?"

Amery declared, "It *will* wait." In three steps he was in Tovin's face, bristling, and Tovin struggled to keep from smiling at the anger that clouded his lover's features. Quietly, so the others wouldn't overhear, the regent asked, "Are you all right?"

"Fine," Tovin whispered. He glanced past Amery to frown at Giles, who had abandoned the sparring field to join their friends at the table. "We can discuss this later. They're watching us."

"Let them," Amery muttered. "Am I not the regent here? Can I not inquire after the health of my best knight?"

Tovin felt a smile tug at his lips. "We were fighting for that title," he admitted, sheathing his sword. "I have not yet won it." He raised his voice to add, "If that coward Giles would be so kind as to return to the pitch, perhaps we can fight on."

"No." Avery turned to glare at his other knights, as if a look from him alone could prevent their match. "I forbid it."

Absently, the regent reached out, his hand finding the chipped links in Tovin's armor where Giles's sword had cut. Even through the chain mail, Tovin felt his blood surge at the touch. He closed his eyes, imagining the two of them alone, the armor gone between them and those fingers trailing over ticklish flesh…

Then he remembered their friends, *damn* it, and Tovin swatted that hand away. "Amery," he warned. Before the regent could reply, Tovin stormed past him to the conference table, a scowl twisting his face in anger. Throwing himself into an empty chair, he glared at Amery, a challenge shining in his eyes. "Well? What is it you needed to tell us that couldn't *possibly* wait until our contest was over?"

NOT FOR THE first time, Amery wished he could put an end to the charade between himself and Sir Tovin. When Giles's sword had struck true, he could've sworn the blade cut deep into his own body, he *felt* it. Without caring what the others would think, he'd rushed to Tovin's side, gathered him in his arms, held him as close as he could...

But his knight's mind had been on the others. Tovin was always careful around their friends, around anyone. Why couldn't Amery take the knight into his arms and not worry who said what? Was he not the regent? Wasn't his word law?

Then why could he not love whom he wanted? Why could a simple knight like Berik flaunt his sexuality while the regent himself had to curb his desires? His father had tried time and again to explain to him why he must keep himself aloof from love, his heart unfettered to any one person. The people needed a regent they could rally behind, a warrior in whom they could trust. Lying with another man just to satisfy a sexual need was frowned upon amid the lower classes, and unheard of among the gentry. In his father's eyes, why Amery would choose to rut with a man like some sort of barbaric animal when there were women enough willing to be queened for a night in the regent's bed threatened the very fabric of his existence.

Amery could still recall with vivid detail the night his father had called for him. The young prince had just turned eighteen, a fact he'd celebrated days earlier by finally giving himself to Tovin. It had been special, loving, the culmination of years of unspoken desire, and since that moment, Amery couldn't be bothered to think of anyone other than the fair knight, with his long curls, his dark eyes, his thick cock...

The stern mask on his father's face curbed those thoughts. Amery knew this would not be a pleasant discussion. Without preamble, King Adin announced, "I forbid you to frolic with that knight."

Surprised to find his father's words mirroring his own sordid thoughts, Amery started, "I don't—"

"Sir Tovin." Each word was succinct, clipped, as if the king wanted nothing more than to cut them from his vocabulary completely. "You'll not see him again."

"He's my friend."

Twin spots of bright red rose to color the king's cheeks. "I have heard otherwise. You'd do well to keep your hosen on and your breeches tied, boy, if you plan to assume the throne one day. I'll not have a scandal in my castle, nor in the stables, either."

Amery flushed with embarrassment. How much did his father know? That he'd been in the stables with Tovin, obviously. The day before, the two of them had snuck away from the others to lie together in the loft above the horses. The hay provided a soft bed beneath Amery's back, and he'd gripped one of the worn ceiling beams, biting the wood like a cribbing horse to stifle his cries of pleasure when Tovin finally entered him. Closing his eyes, Amery remembered the touch of strong hands on his hips, the feel of Tovin's thickness filling his ass, the heated rhythm they found and the heady kisses that followed their simultaneous orgasm.

Cutting easily into that memory, the king prodded, "Son? Do you understand me?"

Amery had to bite the inside of his lip to keep from railing in anger against his father's stubborn, ignorant words. His hands clenched into fists behind his back as he struggled to keep his voice neutral. "Yes, Your Majesty. I understand completely. I shall no longer be a *friend* to Sir Tovin."

Silently, he added, *I shall become so much more, old man, and neither you nor the people of Pharr shall stop me.*

CHAPTER 3

WHEN AMERY BROKE the news to Tovin, his friend shocked him by laughing.

"What the hell can you possibly find so damn funny about this?" the prince demanded. They lay together on the divan in his quarters, Tovin stretched out beneath him, both anxiously glancing at the chamber door in case a servant appeared unannounced. "My life is over. If I can't have you—"

But Tovin had tousled Amery's hair, ruffling the normally smooth surface of that auburn curtain. Though Amery shooed him away, he couldn't help but grin at the touch. "So we'll simply no longer be friends," Tovin explained.

Amery didn't understand why the knight's voice sounded so...so *happy* at the thought. A world without Tovin seemed bleak and lifeless. How would he get through the day? "I shall plunge a dagger into my heart," he announced with all the seriousness of a teenager in love. "I shall pluck out my eyes, and cut off my hands, and—"

"Both of them?" Tovin teased. At the tortured look that flickered across Amery's face, he kissed the prince's nose. "If you cut off one, what will you use to hold the knife to sever the other?"

Amery sighed. "Stop being so contrary. I cannot live without you."

"You did well enough before we met," Tovin pointed out.

His slight smile was infuriating. Sitting up, Amery straightened his disheveled coverlet and tried to look as callous as Tovin's words sounded to him. He struggled to choke back hot tears that blinded him. "Why must you be so cruel? I *love* you."

Tovin pushed himself up from the divan and leaned his chin on Amery's shoulder. "And I you," he whispered, "more than you know. But if your father forbids it—"

"Fuck my father," Amery spat.

He felt Tovin grin against his ear. "I don't really want to," he teased. One arm came up around Amery's thin waist. "I'd much rather fuck you."

"We can't." Amery's voice came out strangled. "He said—"

"We can't be friends," Tovin whispered.

Amery nodded; in his chest, his heart felt as if it would burst, and his whole body began to shake with desire at Tovin's closeness, at the arm around his waist, the breath soft in his ear. In anguish, his hands twisted in his coverlet.

Tovin's voice dipped lower, filling Amery up inside. "So we won't be."

The prince started, but Tovin held him tight, leaning against him as if to hold him still. "Not out loud," he added. Amery let his words sink in. "What we have will be shared only between the two of us, my prince. Let the world see what they need to. Their opinion will never change who you are to me."

Thus, their public feud had begun.

✦

WHEN THE KING disappeared, Amery was not immediately crowned in his place. The royal vizier and his advisors thought it best if the young prince was named regent, on the slim chance that King Adin returned. Amery thought it unlikely—his father was a warrior first, and if his shield had fallen unclaimed to the battlefield, it fell from lifeless hands. But two years had passed since the shield had been found, and there was no further word from the enemy to give hope that Adin might still be alive. The advisors were beginning to believe that a ceremony to crown the new king might be just the encouragement the people needed to continue fighting the invaders from the north.

Taking the crown meant choosing a queen. Dozens of young women haunted the castle courtyard, hoping to catch the prince's eye, but Amery had thus far successfully managed to avoid them all. But becoming king meant he had to marry; it meant producing an heir, becoming a father, and leaving Tovin behind.

Amery did not think he could sacrifice so much for the common good.

But the crowning was only so much talk at the moment—the real threat were the Cyrians from the north. Every day, reports came in from the battlefield, more ground lost, more lives taken, more men dead beneath the barbarians' blades. Rumor had it that their steel was tipped in a poison so strong, it refused to allow the blood to clot or skin to heal. A simple nick in the armor was enough to bleed a man to death. Daily, the number of soldiers who fell on the front lines was rivaled by the number of deserters who left their posts out of fear.

And recent runners brought with them news that the battle was advancing on the castle. In desperation, Amery had decided to call home the four knights who commanded his troops.

Now they sat before him, the three boys he loved as brothers and the one he loved much, much more. Taking his place at the head of the table, Amery studied each of the knights in turn, letting his gaze linger on Tovin. The sweat beading his lover's skin, dampening his forehead and tightening his curls, only added to his beauty. Amery didn't want to put him in danger—didn't want *any* of them hurt. With a sigh, the regent admitted, "I've called you here because the northern border is crumbling. The Cyrians threaten to break through our defenses any day now—"

"We *know* this," Tovin said, exasperated. He was still sore at losing to Giles, and probably a bit frustrated because the others' presence prevented any real reunion with Amery. The regent's own feelings were just as stymied. Tovin refused to meet Amery's gaze, instead turning to their friend as he asked, "Berik's got that covered, don't you?"

Berik, in command of the kingdom's northern forces, gave a noncommittal shrug. "They're a strong race," he said. "But my men try to keep them at bay."

"Rumor has it they've gained the river." Amery fixed Berik with a steady stare. Berik shrugged again. "If they pass the forest—"

"Oh, they won't," Berik assured him. "Trust me, Your Highness. My men will prevail."

"Sounds like your men are failing," Tovin pointed out with a derisive snort. When Berik glared at him, Tovin smirked. "Is that why we're here? To pick up the slack?"

"You're here," Amery told them, "because I need to consolidate our forces if we're going to drive these bastards from the kingdom. Lohden—"

The knight looked up from his book; the intense look on his face proved that he'd been following the conversation, however engrossed he'd seemed to be in his studies. "My men are at your command, Your Highness."

With a smile of thanks, the regent said, "They're heading east. I want you to cut them off at the druid ruins. Berik, you follow him."

"What about the westlands?" Berik wanted to know. "The fight's hot and heavy there. My men are scattered pretty thin across the northern border. If I shift them east, I leave the west open to attack."

Amery just shook his head. "Giles has the west. Tovin, station your men here, around the castle—"

"What the hell?" Tovin cried.

Amery frowned at the indignation he heard in his lover's voice. How long had he spent mulling over this plan? Watching himself in the mirror of his father's shield as he made the suggestion to keep Tovin here—he'd said the words over and over again until they slipped from his lips without a hint of the passion that underlay them. Of all the men in his military, Tovin was the best. That alone was reason to assign him as castellan of the kingdom's seat. Hoping his voice didn't betray his other reason for wanting Tovin close, Amery explained, "I need you here with me."

The look in Tovin's eyes was hard to meet. "No way," he announced. "I'm the best knight you have and you know it. Send me to the front. I'll turn those half-bred bastards around and have them scurrying back to their frozen wasteland in no time."

"No," Amery replied. The thought of his lover in battle was too much for him—he couldn't think of it, *wouldn't*. He'd almost died when Giles's sword cut through Tovin's mail earlier; how would Amery survive knowing it was he who'd sent Tovin into the thick of battle? "I need you *here*. What if the Cyrians get this far? Who will protect the throne?"

Who'll protect me? Amery almost added, but he bit his lip before the words could escape. "Tovin…" He didn't know if Tovin's protests were legit or if his lover merely balked because they had an audience. "I need troops stationed here. I need a castellan to oversee our fortifications—"

Tovin rose to his feet in anger. "You know I'd prevail against those barbarians. I'd have them beat in no time." His deep voice thundered dangerously across the table. "I never thought you'd be one to let your personal feelings for me come before what's best for your kingdom."

The entire world seemed to stop at Tovin's words. *Don't say it*, Amery prayed, but part of him wanted Tovin to come out with it, *wanted* the words to be free. Then there would be no charade, no play-acting, no lies between them. The other knights watched them argue, fascinated; even Lohden pulled his nose out of his book for the occasion.

Amery met Tovin's heated gaze and could see their lives

hanging in the balance within those dark blue depths. On one hand, freedom to love as they would; on the other, this continued farce. Don't, Amery thought. *Please don't.*

But if you do, I swear I will still stand beside you.

Then something in Tovin's eyes dulled, and Amery knew the knight had lost his nerve. For all his strength and bravery, admitting their affair proved beyond Tovin's ability.

The regent sighed, more disappointed than he would have thought he'd be. As if he had never hesitated, Tovin continued his rant, choosing the safe route and keeping their secret between the two of them alone. "You don't like me?" the knight asked. "Fine. You want to argue and fight and bitch at me? *Fine.* But you're jeopardizing your people, *regent,* if you keep me from the front. You *know* that. I am their best defense—"

"What is best for my people," Amery spat, bitter, "is that their regent lives. And if you are the best damn knight I have, then you'll see it is your sworn duty to protect me. *Me.* This castle is where you're needed, Sir Tovin. This *castle* is where you'll stay."

"I don't—" Tovin started.

Weary, Amery cut him off. "I'll not argue it further."

Turning from the table, he stalked across the room and called back over his shoulder to the other knights, "Berik, Lohden, the two of you leave for the eastern front at first light. Giles heads west." At the door he stared back at them, at *Tovin,* and growled, "Send for your men, Tovin. You're stationed here."

"Damn it the hell," Tovin muttered, loud enough for the regent to hear. With a frustrated growl, he yanked off his gauntlets and threw them onto the table, where they clattered heavily against the solid wood.

Amery suppressed a grin as he left the drawing room.

✦

TO HONOR THE knights' arrival at the castle, dinner was a feast held in the large dining hall rarely graced with the regent's presence. Amery usually took his meals in his own chambers, away from the gossip and giggles of the courtesans who at times almost seemed an extension of the castle itself. Young women flocked to the castle dinners, hoping to catch the regent's eye; mingled among their number were citizens with grievances they wanted aired, or commoners looking for free handouts, or politically minded men who wanted to bend Amery's ear with their own biased views. He would much rather avoid the whole lot and eat alone.

Or with Sir Tovin. *That* would have been nice.

But he could think of no excuse as to why the knight had to join him in his own chambers, just him and no others. Or rather, no excuse that wouldn't raise suspicions. He would have to wait until later in the evening before he could get the knight alone, and let his touch and his kisses soothe Tovin's wounded pride.

He hated waiting.

During the meal, Amery sat in the middle of a long banquet table, perched on an ornate chair that grew uncomfortable as the evening lagged. On either side of him sat his advisors, men who had been his father's before him, and who still spoke of King Adin in the present tense, as if his disappearance were nothing more than an extended trip to the far reaches of his kingdom. These same men had recently begun to poison Amery's mind with talk of taking the crown and, with it, a wife.

Even now, as they ate from the roast boar set before the regent's plate, they dropped salacious hints about a ceremony. "The populace needs direction," Mordrent said to no one in particular. The eldest of the advisors, he sat at Amery's right hand and often gripped the young prince's arm with spindly fingers to drive his point home. "At this moment in time, with the Cyrians practically crossing our moat, the people need encouragement. It is your duty to give them hope. If they could but see the crown again—"

"I cannot wear it in battle," Amery replied. He pulled his arm away from Mordrent's groping hand before the old man could snatch it. "Once this present threat has passed, I will consider it."

From Amery's other side, a woman laughed. Bellona was the only female advisor on his staff, a proud woman, never married, childless, who carried herself with a regal, almost haughty air. Her gray hair shone like the silver wires she wore twisted up among her curls. She had been a fixture at the castle for as long as Amery could remember—the faint memories of his own mother, a frail woman who died before he was seven, sometimes mingled with his thoughts of Bellona, creating one formidable matron in his mind.

"Consider?" Bellona asked, her voice thick with disapproval. One finely drawn eyebrow rose on the porcelain skin of her face, and when she turned toward Amery, the look he saw in her icy eyes made him squirm. "You *are* the regent, Your Highness," she pointed out. "You *will* take the crown. Only death would release you from your obligation."

If all women were as ruthless and conniving as Bellona, Amery thought, he sure as *hell* didn't plan to marry. Death would be preferable…but her cold gaze stemmed any snide comment he may have made. With difficulty, he swallowed the food in his mouth and looked away.

His gaze trailed down the tables that abutted his—they formed a U-shape, his table connecting the others. On his left side, the chairs were filled with breathless, giggling beauties, busy picking over their plates and fanning ample bosoms that strained at the seams in their dresses. One of the women saw him looking and elbowed the girl beside her; soon the whole table smiled in his direction, eyes winking, jewelry flashing, petite hands tipped with polished nails fluttering at him in greeting.

Amery groaned and bent over his plate, focusing on the food he shoveled into his mouth. From the corner of his vision, he glanced at the table on his right, where his knights sat. The four friends roared with laughter, knocking their goblets together in raucous toasts, joking with the men beside them, living it up, and Amery would have given half his kingdom to be able to join them without reproach.

Lohden's ever-present book had been put away; he and Giles tossed pellets of bread down the length of the table, snickering when their makeshift missiles struck someone. Berik leaned against the young squire beside him—from the kid's flushed cheeks and hooded eyes, Amery could imagine all too well where Berik's large hand had settled beneath the table. Narrowing his eyes, the regent glared at the squire and considered throwing him from the hall, from the castle even, if only for the crime of doing what he wanted when the regent could not.

Beside them sat Tovin. The knight grinned at his friends' antics, but every now and then that dark gaze flickered Amery's way. Tovin's face was an impenetrable mask, and Amery could read nothing in the depths of his stormy eyes. The regent's body ached for his knight's touch—why couldn't he sit beside Tovin like the squire who leaned into Berik? Then Tovin's strong hand would be curving around Amery's thigh, easing into the draws of his breeches, fumbling over the erection that had woken at the sound of the trumpet declaring Tovin's arrival.

Here in the dining hall, there were too many shadows between himself and the knight, too many people. He wanted to be sitting beside Tovin, right here, right now, to gaze into those beautiful eyes and hear that breathy laugh whisper inside him. He should be able to lean against Tovin, feel that warm body alongside his, reach up and run his fingers through the damp curls that tumbled to the knight's collar. It wasn't fair—

A cold hand touched his wrist. Amery jerked as if caught staring and turned to find Bellona watching him, her perfectly painted lips pursed in thought. "You *do* want the crown, Your Highness," she purred. "Do you not?"

What he wanted was Tovin, but until the feast was over and they could be alone, the knight would remain out of his reach. Meeting Bellona's steady gaze, Amery threw her previous comment back at her in reply. "Only death would keep me from it."

CHAPTER 4

WHEN THE MEAL was over, Amery found himself pinned down by his guests, who took advantage of the regent's presence to besiege him with questions he would rather have answered during the weekly sessions he held in the throne room. He watched, helpless, as his knights rose from their table and excused themselves from the dining hall. Only Tovin paused to glance back, his face closed, his eyes unreadable.

Then the crowd surged toward the middle table, and Tovin's friends pulled him from view.

When Amery finally managed to escape, he found Tovin in the now empty drawing room, brooding. From the doorway, he studied his lover, who sat at the table where the knights had gathered to hear the regent's news. A slight frown graced Tovin's face as he picked at the gauntlets he'd thrown down earlier.

So beautiful, Amery thought, taking in the sandy curls that accented smooth skin tanned to the color of roasted almonds. Tovin had always been a handsome boy, but time and his long absences from the castle only increased his good looks in Amery's opinion. The regent allowed himself a heart-felt sigh that announced his presence.

Tovin's deep-sea eyes flashed like storm clouds overhead when he turned. "I was beginning to wonder if you would ever leave the feast."

Closing the door, Amery crossed the room to stand behind the knight. He rested a hand on Tovin's mail-covered shoulder and couldn't stop it from trailing down the length of the mail covering Tovin's arm. "Did you win?"

He referred to the knights' earlier contest, their sparring to see who among them was the best. Tovin laughed, a short, breathy sound. "Of course."

Moving his hand back to Tovin's shoulder, Amery worked his fingers through the chinks in his lover's armor to give him an affectionate squeeze, then caressed the soft skin of his lover's exposed neck. "Fence with me, then," he suggested. "I'm good with a sword."

But Tovin caught Amery's hand in his and tugged until the regent stepped around the chair to stand before him. There was nothing unreadable in his gaze now—those eyes smoldered with a fiery lust that fanned the flames in Amery's own blood. "How can I fight you?" Tovin asked as he wrapped his arms around Amery's waist. He leaned his head against the regent's stomach and sighed. "It's my duty to protect you. I'll not put you in danger."

With a laugh, Amery ran his hands through Tovin's thick hair. Fisting into the curly length, he gave a gentle tug and pointed out, "You'd do well to remember that."

Tovin looked up at him, a questioning look on his face.

Amery gave him a sad smile. "You fought me every step of the way this afternoon. The servants say we quarrel too much."

"Their talk is the reason we bicker," Tovin teased with a wink.

The regent let out a lusty sigh. "Is there nothing better for the scullery maids to discuss than who I bring into my bed?"

"It's breaking news," Tovin joked. As Amery's hand rubbed over the top of his head, Tovin's eyes slipped shut and he leaned back, chin resting against Amery's coverlet, lips puckering as he blew a kiss at the arm stretched out above him. "Some would rather gossip about your love life, or lack thereof, than worry about the northern invaders."

"I have a very lively love life," Amery objected. "Thank you very much."

Tovin opened one eye, mouth twisted in a sardonic grin. "Oh, you do?" he asked. "Even when I'm not here?" A dull blush crept into Amery's face, and Tovin winked. "So tell me, Your Highness, which hand thou dost prefer?"

With a loud *hrumph*, Amery smacked the top of Tovin's head. "Hush. Or you will spend tonight in the stocks after all, I'll warrant."

Both eyes opened now. Looking up at his lover, Tovin drew his lips down into a pretty pout that made Amery's stomach flutter. "I love you," he admitted. "I wish this farce would end already. Sometimes I just want to crush you in my arms and cover you with kisses, and I can't. I have to wait until we're alone, and I *hate* waiting."

"I know."

With a suggestive smile, Amery sank to his knees, his hand slipping from the knight's curls to trail down over his cheek. Tovin leaned into the touch and lowered his face to keep Amery in sight. Now it was the regent who looked up into *his* eyes. His voice lowered to an intimate level when he whispered, "We're alone now."

"So we are." Tovin leaned forward to kiss Amery, whose eyes closed in anticipation.

But those sweet lips never touched his. Tovin hissed, a sharp intake of breath, and when Amery looked, he saw his lover wincing at a sudden pain in his side. "Gods," he gasped, pressing a hand against the broken chinks in his armor where Giles's sword had bit into him during battle.

Concern flashed across Amery's face. "Let me see," he commanded, brushing Tovin's hand away.

Tovin protested, "I'm fine."

But he let Amery help ease off his armored mail and the surcoat beneath it. The regent caught his breath at the sight of his lover's bare chest, the muscles well defined, the smooth skin hairless except for tufts of faint curls that clung to Tovin's ruddy nipples. Though the fight had been hours ago, there was still an angry red mark along Tovin's side, and a thin scratch marred the skin below his nipple where Giles's blade slashed at him. "Damn," Tovin muttered, picking at the dried blood. "I didn't think he got me. The old bastard must've learned a thing or two since we sparred last."

"I hope it doesn't scar." Before Tovin could stop him, Avery leaned forward and kissed the cut.

The knight caught his breath as Amery's lips tickled his skin; one hand smoothed over the regent's thick, soft hair.

"Oh, Tovin," Amery sighed. He hugged his lover gently, mindful of the wound. Tovin's skin was warm against his cheek, and he felt more than heard the strong beat of Tovin's heart. "I don't want to lose you. How will I go on if you die? Tell me that."

Tovin laughed, a low, vibrant sound that rumbled through Amery and made the regent hug him tighter. "You'd find a way," he promised.

But Amery shook his head stubbornly. "I don't *want* to find a way. I want you." With a sigh, he added, "You were right. It's selfish of me to keep you here, but I can't bear the thought of you on the front, so far away from me…I'll be so *lonely.*"

"Can't have that, now can we?" Tovin teased. When Amery looked up at him, the knight leaned down and kissed the corner of his mouth. Amery's hands caressed Tovin's flat stomach and muscular chest, tracing the curves of his body as if relearning them after all the time they'd spent apart. It had been too damn long.

Finally he reached up, hands cupped around Tovin's neck, thumbs rubbing the sensitive skin behind his lover's ears as he pulled him down for another kiss, a *real* kiss. Tovin's mouth opened, his breath warm on Amery's upper lip. The regent caught Tovin's lower lip between his teeth, then moaned as his tongue licked into the knight, rediscovering the taste of him. It was a gentle kiss at first, probing, tentative.

Then Tovin shifted in his seat and pressed Amery back against the table behind him. Their lips met in a velvet crush. *This* was what they'd both been waiting for, *this*…since the last time Tovin had been at the castle, Amery had ached for this touch, these lips, this mouth on his, this sweetness he tasted in his sleep and yearned for throughout the day.

When Tovin tried to pull away, Amery's hands fisted in his hair, keeping him close. It took a dozen little kisses before the regent would release him. Breathless, the knight teased, "So you'd risk the kingdom's safety because you don't want to be lonely?"

"I'd miss you." Amery pulled Tovin to him again, mouth covering the knight's to claim another kiss. Against his lips, Amery whispered, "I wasn't kidding when I mentioned making you castellan. You'd command the castle guard. We'd never have to sleep apart."

"And the servants would talk," Tovin reminded him.

Amery sighed, exasperated. "Let them," he snapped. "I'm the regent. Do they not want me to be happy?"

Tovin smoothed down Amery's sleek hair and didn't reply. Amery knew his lover had heard it before—whenever they managed to get together, he always started in on how unfair it was they had to keep their love a secret, how they had to fight to dissuade rumors, how he would be so much happier if they could just stay together forever and the rest of the kingdom, the rest of the *world*, be damned. The mock feud between the regent and his knight had begun when King Adin still ruled the land, but that man was gone. Could laws not be changed? Why did Amery *have* to abide by his father's word?

But though he was loathe to admit it, there *was* some sense of duty in him that held his tongue. He had been raised for the throne, and trained to keep the kingdom in mind at all times. Much as he wanted to be nothing more than a man in love, he knew in his heart that as long as the threat of the crown hovered above him like a halo just beyond his reach, he would never be free. Or happy…

Amery closed his eyes in frustration and pressed his lips to Tovin's. "You make me happy," he whispered. "Don't fight with the others. Gods, if Giles was half the swordsman you are, if his sword had dug a mite deeper…"

"Don't think that," Tovin told him. "I'm fine." Cradling Amery's face in his hands, he stared into his eyes and smiled. "I *am* fine, really. More so now that you're here with me—"

Behind them the door scraped open. Amery stumbled backwards in his haste to pull away from Tovin and cracked his head against the table behind him. "Fuck," he muttered as he stood.

Tugging his coverlet into place, he glared at the young page who entered the room. "Do you not knock?" he demanded, his voice sharper than it needed to be. But they'd almost been caught—why had he not locked the door behind him when he entered? What had the boy seen? *Almost…*

The page looked at Tovin's bare chest and frowned. "Your Highness," he gasped. "Sir Tovin. I did not know…"

Tovin sighed, weary. "What is it?" Amery snapped again.

As the page's gaze flickered over him, Amery raised a hand to smooth down his hair and hoped the heat in his cheeks didn't give him away. "Sir Lohden is looking for you," the boy said. "Your Highness, is everything—"

"Fine," Amery said, thinking quickly. "Sir Tovin was wounded earlier."

"I'm not—" Tovin started.

Amery ignored him. "I want a physician in here at once."

Taking another step away from Tovin, the regent toyed absently with the knight's surcoat, discarded on the table. He seemed unable to raise his eyes to look at the page—all he saw was Tovin's naked chest, and the knight's taste was still sharp in his mouth. But when he realized the page was still in the room, he pushed the surcoat out of reach with a scowl. "Well?" he asked, impatient to be alone again. "He shall bleed to death while you stand there gawking. What are you waiting for? A royal decree?"

The boy scurried from the room. "Wait!" Tovin cried out, rising to his feet, but the page was already gone. Turning to show Amery the sword's scratch, he added, "I'm not bleeding. I don't need a physician and you know it."

Amery shrugged. "What else was I supposed to say?" he wanted to know. "You're half dressed. You said yourself the servants talk."

Glancing at the open door, he sighed. He wanted to touch Tovin again, to kiss him and feel his strong hands on his body, but he couldn't chance it, not now. "I love you," he whispered. His lips barely moved as he said the words.

Tovin smiled and leaned in close, until Amery's coverlet brushed against his bare chest with each trembling breath. Amery's whole body ached to span the inch that separated them, to take his lover into his arms and never let him go, but he couldn't do that, he just couldn't.

Then Tovin whispered into his ear, his deep voice like that of a breathless ghost. "One hour," he promised.

Outside the room, footsteps rang in the stone hall, and Amery knew he should move away, they shouldn't be seen like this, but his body wouldn't obey and he let Tovin's hot breath curl through him, warming a path from his ear to his groin. "I'll meet you in your chambers then. Tell the servants you don't wish to be disturbed."

As the page entered the room again, Tovin turned from Amery and gathered up his armor and surcoat from the table. "I don't need medical attention," Tovin told the boy. "The regent here is just over-reacting."

Amery's face flushed from the memory of Tovin's closeness. To cover his emotions, he replied hotly, "I am *not* over-reacting!"

The physician entered the room behind the page. A young

woman a few years Tovin's senior, she flashed them a bright but harried smile. "You're wounded?" she asked, as if the thought made her day.

Tovin shook his head. "I'm fine," he said again. "Just a flesh wound. Nothing more."

Without looking at Amery, he strode from the room, brushing between the page and the physician. After a moment's hesitation, the physician dropped a quick curtsey at the regent, then scurried after the knight.

Amery smirked when he heard her call after Tovin to slow down, let her take a look. Then he noticed his page, waiting to be addressed, and he remembered the boy's reason for interrupting them. Scowling, he prompted, "Sir Lohden?"

One hour, he thought. *Then he'll be mine. Finally.* He didn't know if he could wait that much longer.

CHAPTER 5

AN HOUR LATER, Tovin slipped through the castle halls to the regent's chambers. The castle guard recognized the knight and didn't question him. The commander of the kingdom's southern troops, Tovin was well known among the guard, who had heard of his being stationed at the castle. Those who saw him pass on his way to Amery's rooms assumed he was going to argue that command with the regent yet again. With Sir Tovin in residence, the regent's mood had steadily deteriorated throughout the evening, until servants and guards alike began to hurry out of the way whenever Amery approached, glowering. They avoided Tovin altogether, which suited the knight just fine.

At Amery's door, he didn't even knock. The door opened easily, as he knew it would, and he closed it quietly behind him when he entered. *I've been waiting too long,* he thought as he crossed the sitting room on the way to the bed chamber. *Maybe he's right. Maybe I should let him reassign me here, where I can see him every day, and love him every night.*

In the bedroom he stopped at the doorway, speechless. The regent's oversized bed stood on a dais, commanding most of the room, and was covered in rich teal sheets, its pillows and comforter crafted from a shimmering fabric that alternated between teal and a deep bronze depending on the light. The regent's crest was embroidered in a golden brocade on the pillows, but the fall of dark auburn hair spread across the pillows obscured much of their design. Amery lay on his back above the covers, his long hair fanned out around him, his slim body nude.

Candles flickered around the room, casting a golden glow on the regent's skin, burnishing the knot of red hair curled at his groin, igniting a fire deep within his light green eyes. His slim body still retained much of its boyish characteristics—the hairless chest, the clusters of freckles that dotted his pale flesh, the narrow hips, the lithe legs. But the thick, uncut length that hung between those legs was a man's cock, and Tovin's own dick stirred in his breeches at the sight of Amery's glorious shaft.

As he watched, the regent's long fingers strummed over his flat stomach, over the slight mound of his pubic bone, then down along his cock. Beneath the feathery touch, his dick stirred like a beast roused from slumber; Tovin saw it twitch and could feel the shudder that ran through Amery at his own touch. Then the plum-colored knob poked from under the foreskin, pre-cum already beading on its tip.

"Well?" The regent's voice was low, intimate between them, but Tovin jumped at the suddenness of it. "Will you join me?" Amery asked, "or would you rather watch?"

Without reply, Tovin shed his armor covering and swallowed against the lust rising in him as he approached the bed. Amery watched him with hooded bedroom eyes that smoldered like coals, his lips curved into a sexy half-smile. One thought flittered through Tovin's mind...*Did I lock the door?*

Almost immediately, he answered, *Who cares?* There was no way he was going back, not now. Let the kingdom fall during the night, let the castle walls tumble down around them, let King Adin himself come back from the dead and tear through the door to the regent's chambers, Tovin didn't care. All that mattered at the moment was taking the man before him into his arms, pressing as much of his bare skin to Amery's as he could, and diving so deep within the regent that he never surfaced again.

"Gods," he breathed as he crawled onto Amery.

The regent started to speak, but Tovin covered his mouth with his own, silencing him with a hungry kiss as his hands roamed the smooth body beneath him. His fingers plucked Amery's nipples erect, eliciting gasps of delight from his lover. Moving lower, he brushed away the hand at Amery's crotch and grasped the thick length, massaging it in his fist, working it hard.

"Tovin," Amery managed to murmur between kisses. When Tovin cupped his balls and tickled one forefinger along the tender skin behind them, the regent arched into the knight's body and moaned. "It's been too long."

Straddling Amery's hips, Tovin sat back and pulled off his surcoat. "It has," he agreed with a grin.

The regent reached for him, hands tugging at the scant hair on his chest, then thumbing over his nipples. Each touch sent a sliver of pleasure spiking through Tovin like lightning, striking his overly sensitive nipples and shooting down to stir the blood already thickening in his dick. He could come from such play—one of the first times he and Amery had been together, when they were still teenagers and kissing was the extent of their lovemaking, Amery had been amused to find that a few minutes' suckling on Tovin's teats was more than enough to get him off.

Catching Amery's hands in his, Tovin raised them to his mouth and kissed each fingertip. "Stop that," he admonished, "or I won't be able to pierce that sexy ass of yours with my sword."

Amery laughed and, twisting one hand free from Tovin's grip, poked at the bulge in the front of the knight's breeches. "Your sword? Is *that* what this is? Unsheathe it, knight, and wield it for me. Let me test its breadth and heft. Let me feel its blade."

Tovin rocked back, his buttocks pressing Amery's hard cock under them. The regent's mocking words dissolved in a gasp of delight as his eyes shut against the sensations caused by

Tovin's body against his. The hand at Tovin's crotch bunched in the fabric covering his erection with a gentle squeeze that made him moan.

Catching that hand again, Tovin raised it to the other and held both of Amery's wrists to his chest. "I have an idea," he announced.

"What's that?" Amery wiggled his hips beneath Tovin to remind him that he was waiting for something more. "Can you tell me later?"

Tovin laughed. "I can tell you now," he replied. "I'm still mostly dressed. These pants aren't coming off until I'm ready."

Amery pouted and tried to twist his wrists free from Tovin's grip. "I think you're ready now," he declared. "I'm the regent. My word is law. I say you're ready."

Laughing again, Tovin leaned down over the regent, stretching his lover's hands above his head to keep them out of reach. Amery's nipples brushed Tovin's; he had to close his eyes against the thrill sparked by that touch. Between them, his cock throbbed in his pants, aching for release.

"I think you're in no position to argue with me now," he whispered, touching the tip of Amery's nose with his own. Amery leaned up for a kiss but Tovin pulled away slightly. "Not yet."

Amery sighed, frustrated. "Kiss me now. I demand it."

"You can't make demands here," Tovin told him. Squeezing his wrists gently, he kissed Amery's cheek, just a flutter of his lips against the soft skin. When Amery turned to catch the kiss on his mouth, however, Tovin pulled away again. "You're not doing this right."

Exasperated, Amery said, "Then tell me your idea already, will you? Tell me so we can get on with this. Please?" When Tovin didn't reply, he added, "I'll beg if you want me to."

Tovin thought it over. The image of Amery on his knees, naked and begging to be loved, was almost too much to bear. "Much as I like the way that sounds," Tovin said, kissing

Amery's chin as his lover whimpered, "I'll not make you beg. Not tonight."

Amery tried to kiss Tovin, but the knight pulled away as his lover's lips brushed against his jaw. "Tovin," Amery whined, and Tovin laughed. "This isn't fun."

"This is a lot of fun," Tovin argued. He slid down a little, grinding his hips into Amery's, until their erections pressed together with a sweet ache. "Don't you want to hear my idea?"

"Will you love me after you tell me?" Amery wanted to know.

Without warning, Tovin kissed Amery greedily, his lips parting Amery's own as his tongue eased into his lover's waiting mouth. Amery moaned, breathless, and arched into Tovin again, trying to twist out of his grip without success. "I love you now," Tovin whispered, trailing tiny kisses down Amery's jaw. He caught Amery's earlobe between his teeth and nipped gently. "Here's my idea."

"What is it?" Amery sighed, his breath a soft rush in Tovin's ear.

Grinning, Tovin whispered, "I think you should reassign me to the castle guard." Then he sat back and winked at Amery. "What do you think? Isn't that brilliant?"

For a moment, the regent stared at him, flabbergasted. Then he struggled against Tovin's tight grip. "Hey! That was *my* idea."

"Yours?" Tovin asked, frowning. "Are you sure?"

The look of consternation that crossed Amery's face made him laugh. Being with the regent allowed him to forget the rest of the world, the northern invaders and the men under his command—every worry he had disappeared when he was with Amery. He kissed the regent's furrowed brow to smooth it out, and Amery kissed his chin, a small peck because he had to strain to reach Tovin. Against Amery's skin, Tovin murmured, "I was so certain it was my idea."

"Tovin," Amery whined again. "This is torture, you know that, right? Pure—"

Tovin cut off the rest of Amery's words with another kiss. Releasing his hands, he caught Amery's cheeks between his palms. *Now* he was ready. The teasing had made them both hard and hungry for each other, and as much as he loved to play, he wanted his man now. Amery fumbled with the drawstring at Tovin's waist in his own eagerness to get them both undressed. "I love you," Amery whispered between kisses, his hands squeezing Tovin's erection through his pants.

Out in the sitting room, a knock sounded on the chamber door.

"Fuck," Tovin whispered. Not now, he thought, struggling to unknot the drawstring. "I thought you told them to leave you alone."

"I did." Anger flashed in Amery's light eyes as Tovin sat up. "I told them—"

The knock came again, louder this time, more insistent. Rolling off Amery, Tovin sighed. "Go see what they want. I'll be here when you get back."

"We can ignore—" Amery started.

Tovin shook his head. "Go," he said. "I'll not be interrupted again. Get rid of them."

✦

WITH A SIGH, Amery pushed himself up from the bed. Beneath his breath, he muttered, "I'll whip whoever it is." The knocking continued, and Amery flounced for the door between his chambers, angry at the interruption. Just when he *finally* had Tovin where he wanted him... *I'll have this servant drawn and quartered for bothering us.* Whipping would be too lenient.

When he reached the doorway, Tovin called out, "You may want to cover yourself, Your Highness. Wouldn't want to terrify the servants."

Amery threw a wicked glare back at his lover, now stretched out on the bed with a smile on his face. "Shut up," he muttered.

But in his sitting room, he paused to grab his dressing robe from where it lay draped over the chaise lounge. As he headed for the door, he cinched the robe about his waist to hide his nakedness. Then he tore open the door, scowling. "What *is* it?"

His page cowered in the hall, one hand raised as if to knock again. Amery glowered down at the boy, who seemed to shrink beneath the weight of his stare. "I told you not to disturb me."

The boy blanched. "It's Sir Giles," he whispered, the words tumbling from his lips in a rush. "He wishes to speak with you—"

Giles. As if anything *he* had to say couldn't wait. Through clenched teeth, Amery growled, "I shall speak with him in the morning."

"But, Your Highness, Sir Giles sent me to fetch you—"

Indignation rose in Amery. He could easily picture the scene—Giles stern as he mimicked the regent, his two friends snickering into their hands. *Fetch me the prince.* That man had *never* showed the first scrap of respect for Amery's position. "I am not a *dog*," the regent spat. "Tell Sir Giles I do not *come* when called."

Part of him wanted to troop down to the guards' quarters and string up Giles on his insubordinate behavior, but that would only be playing into their hands. *It would be a waste of time, teaching that man manners. And Tovin waits.*

Perhaps the knights *knew* where Tovin would be spending the night, or at least suspected. Maybe sending the page was nothing but a little joke designed to interrupt the lovers…

Well, it worked. He pulled the ties of his robe tighter around his waist; let the knights have their laugh—he would have words with Giles in the morning. "Tonight I see no one, do you hear?"

The boy nodded. As Amery started to close the door, he stopped himself and added, "No one. I don't even care if the Cyrians attack—they'll wait until dawn. Is that understood?"

"Yes, Your Highness," the page said quickly. "I'll see to it you aren't disturbed."

"Too late," Amery told him. "Make sure it doesn't happen

a second time or I'll have you demoted to scrubbing out the garderobes."

The boy nodded again, and stepped back as if afraid Amery would snatch him to clean his own latrine this evening. "Yes, Your Highness."

Amery slammed the door shut, cutting off the page's fumbled apology, and threw the lock. On his way back to the bedroom, he discarded the robe, tossing it to the floor. "You best not toy with me again," he called out to Sir Tovin as he entered his bedroom. "I'm in no mood for games. I'll not have it…"

He stopped in midsentence and stared, much in the same manner the knight had when he'd first entered the room. Tovin had used the opportune interruption to remove his boots and breeches, and Amery couldn't take his gaze off his lover. Naked, Tovin lay on his side across the bed, the bare expanse of his skin dusky in the candlelight. With his head propped in one hand, he used his other hand to fondle his swollen penis, squeezing until he moaned. "Tovin," Amery managed, his gaze flickering between that hard cock and the knight's half-lidded eyes.

Tugging on the tip of his erection, Tovin leaned back and whispered, "Come here, my prince."

Amery stumbled on the dais in his haste to reach the bed, but Tovin caught him in strong arms and kissed his trembling lips. "We shall not be disturbed again," Amery promised. "I forbid it."

"So assertive," Tovin sighed. He smoothed a hand down Amery's side, easing the regent back against the bed. "I love that in a ruler. What's this?"

His fingers danced along the length of Amery's dick, teasing it erect. "*My* ruler," Amery laughed. When Tovin's hand closed around it, he leaned back against the pillows and thrust his hips into his lover's grip. "It's twelve if it's an inch."

Tovin's laughter bubbled like sweet champagne between them. "You jest," he murmured, kissing the words into the hollow of Amery's throat. "I'll warrant eight, perhaps. A good length to hold with both hands, to be sure. But twelve would be stretching it."

"I'm the regent," Amery pointed out. "If I say it's twelve..."

His words dissolved into breathy moans as Tovin's fingers slipped below his balls—in his absence, the knight had oiled his hands with some of the perfumed scents Amery kept on the bedside table. He could smell patchouli and musk, and a spicy undercurrent of jasmine that made him feel lethargic and drunk. When Tovin's middle finger rimmed his trembling hole with a gentle motion, leaving an oily trail of perfume behind, Amery clutched at the sheets beneath him and rose off the bed with a shuddery breath. As that finger eased into him, Amery clenched his buttocks, trying to draw it farther in. "Please," he sobbed, writhing beneath Tovin's touch. "Please—"

"Please, what?" Tovin purred.

Amery demanded, "Kiss me." When Tovin didn't comply immediately, he bucked against the finger rimming him and added, "Now."

With a gentle laugh, the knight teased, "You command it?"

Before Amery could reply, Tovin's finger entered him completely, up to the digit's base. But Amery's gasp of delight was smothered by the damp lips that covered his, silencing him in an ardent kiss. The knight's tongue licked into the regent, claiming him, as his finger fucked between Amery's buttocks. Releasing his grip on the bed sheets, Amery raised his hands to cradle Tovin's face and keep his lover close. Where their bodies touched, flames seemed to erupt between them, igniting Amery's flesh and fanning his lust. When their lips parted, he sighed, "Yes, *yes*," the words mere whispers between Tovin's loving kisses.

"Yes, what?" Tovin murmured.

"Take me," Amery begged.

The knight pressed him back to the bed and positioned himself above the regent; Amery spread his legs wide as Tovin guided himself between them. The finger was replaced by the slicked tip of Tovin's cock, and Amery raised his legs to grant his lover entry. "Please," he sighed. He draped his legs around Tovin's hips, crossing his ankles behind the knight's back, squeezing his knees to draw his lover near. "Tovin, please. Love me—"

Another silencing kiss, this one accompanied by a thrust that filled Amery with his lover's hard, thick length. At the sudden burn of entry, the regent's cock spasmed between them, then Tovin leaned Amery back against his pillows, finding a steady rhythm that pushed the rest of the world away. As the knight moved within him, his kisses stole Amery's breath and the regent clung to his lover, arms tight around Tovin's waist, legs clutched around his hips. Together they rocked in the ancient rhythm of love. When his knight finally shoved deep in him and came in a hot rush that filled Amery up inside, the regent climaxed again, leaving them both breathless and satiated.

For the first time in months, Amery felt the weight of his title fall from him as he slept in his lover's tight embrace.

CHAPTER 6

DAWN FOUND THE knights mounted and ready to ride. Tovin stood by Berik's steed and kicked at the cobbled stones. "He has a point," Berik said, nodding at Amery, who spoke with Giles across the courtyard. "You *are* needed here."

Tovin scowled. "I should like the chance to fight. Is that too much to ask?"

Silently, he admitted to himself, *But yes, I would rather stay here.*

Because Berik had indicated Amery, Tovin thought it safe to look at the regent. He avoided doing so in public, unless they were fighting. But the sun was in his eyes, and when he squinted, he could have been looking at anything—Sir Giles perhaps, or the black crow that roosted on a nearby pillar. Shielding his eyes, he watched the way the morning sun sparkled off Amery's hair, turning the dark red into a bright flame. Lust coiled in his stomach and he cleared his throat, turning away before Berik could see the desire in his eyes.

Berik laughed easily and shook the reins free from Tovin's hand. "Be careful," he warned with a grin. "The Cyrians may break through our defense and come knocking on the castle gates. And *then* where would you be? Not so ready to fight, I think."

"Shut up," Tovin growled, but he laughed at his friend's weak attempt at humor.

A thin tension ran through the courtyard like a current sweeping out of the north. Tovin imagined he could hear the clash of swords on the faint breeze that ruffled the horses' manes, and though part of him longed to ride with his friends, he wanted to stay at the castle. He knew he had to—he would trust Amery's safety to no one but himself. Even if it had not been his duty to protect the regent, he would not leave his lover's side. "Kill some of the bastards for me."

"Will do," Berik replied. Spurring his horse, he trotted out of the courtyard.

Lohden's steed fell into step beside Berik's. Tovin laughed to see the book already open in his friend's hand. "What?" Lohden called out with a slow grin. "The horse knows which way to go."

Moments later Giles rode out at a full gallop, headed west to rally his men against the encroaching enemy. Finally two lesser knights left for the southland with orders to retrieve the rest of Tovin's men. Tovin watched them ride out, part of his heart riding with them. He almost didn't hear the faint footsteps that crossed the courtyard to stand behind him. "Well," Amery murmured, his voice suddenly so damn close that Tovin's entire body flushed, "we're alone."

Turning, Tovin gave the regent a brave smile. Amery touched his hand, then pulled away, a furtive gesture that left his skin burning. Keeping his voice low between the two of them, Amery asked, "Would you really want to be reassigned here?"

"We'd never sleep apart," Tovin commented. That thought alone was worth leaving the southland, in his opinion. If he weren't a knight with an army of men who relied on him, he would have moved to the kingdom's seat long ago.

Amery laughed. "Then it's settled. As of today, you command

the castle guard. When this threat is dispersed, you'll stay here."

"The servants should love that," Tovin said with a wink. "We'll kill each other, they'll say."

"Let them talk," Amery replied. He placed a hand on Tovin's shoulder and squeezed gently as they watched their friends disappear in the distance.

✦

LATER THAT EVENING, Amery stormed towards the war room. Those who saw him knew he was going to speak with Sir Tovin, and they scurried out of his way before his wrath could fall on them. All day long, the two had avoided each other, but the servants heard of the knight's reassignment and they feared the arguments to come.

Amery saw the trepidation in his servants' eyes as he passed, but it simply fueled his anger. *If only I could leave this all behind.* It wasn't the first time since his father's death that he wished he could shirk off the duty of his office—he had always suspected the crown wasn't for him. Much as he loved the posh castle life, he couldn't imagine finding someone to share it with, someone who wasn't Tovin. And the kingdom would never allow *that*.

He turned down the corridor that led to the war room, taking the corner a bit too sharply, and bumped into Bellona, whose eyes widened in surprise. "Your Highness," she cried amid the rustle of her skirts.

Some part of Amery wondered if she hadn't been waiting for him. There was something in her demeanor that suggested this encounter had not been left to chance. "Bellona, madam," he said, giving her a curt nod. As she made a show of straightening her dress, he tried to slip around her. Tovin awaited. "If you will excuse me…"

She caught his elbow, her grip surprisingly strong for such a small, feminine hand. Perhaps the weight of the gaudy rings she wore added to her strength. "One moment, Your Highness," she purred.

There was nothing kittenish about her voice—it was the deadly purr of a tiger trying to lull its victim before attack. Amery tried to shake his arm free from her hand, only to feel her nails sink into him like claws. "Bellona," he said again, this time giving her the slight bow he knew she expected. "Please, I must have words with Sir Tovin about the castle's defenses. If you desire an audience—"

"Your father never made me wait."

Bellona's pale gray eyes narrowed as she watched him. Not for the first time, Amery suspected perhaps his father had been bewitched by this woman, with her proud bearing and haughty face. Charmed by her, to be sure, maybe even enamored.

But Amery himself was immune to her feminine wiles, a fact he thought she might already know. Still, she *was* his adviser. He should listen to what she had to say, with or without a scheduled audience. His raging libido would have to wait. Already her presence alone had tamped his sense of urgency. Taking a deep breath, he forced a smile to keep up appearances. "My father was a better man than I," Amery admitted. "But he was never one to make a lady wait, especially one such as yourself."

The grip on his arm relaxed, and Bellona dipped into a quick curtsey. "You honor me with your words."

Amery wanted to scream—were all politics this inane? But he forced his smile wider and told himself to make it quick. "I try. Was there something in particular you wished to discuss?"

His words sounded harsh to his own ears, and Bellona's mouth pursed in thought as she studied him. He resisted the urge to squirm beneath her stare—he was no longer a little boy caught running in the corridors; he was *regent*. The thought straightened his spine a bit, drawing him up to his full height.

Bellona noticed. "Your Highness," she murmured, pulling his arm to her and ensconcing it with both her own. She cuddled up to him as if they were old friends, and he resisted the urge to move away.

But when she spoke, she lowered her voice, forcing him to lean closer to hear what she had to say. "I know you have a lot on your mind right now," she told him, patting his arm in a motherly way that he found very distracting. "But I believe you should seriously consider assuming the crown—"

With an exasperated sigh, Amery cried, "I don't have the time—"

"The people need you," Bellona continued. When he tried to wrest free from her grip, she only held on tighter. "They need to see someone leading them to battle, not cowering behind his knights. They need a figurehead."

"They need a martyr." Amery shook his head. "I'll not do it, Bellona. I cannot make such a decision at this point in time. It's the rest of my life you're talking about here. I can't just rush into it—"

"Who's rushing you?" Bellona wanted to know.

You, for starters. But Amery kept that thought to himself.

At his silence, she pointed out, "You've known since birth that you would rule over Pharr. It's time to put away your boyhood, Amery, and I say this in the gentlest way possible, but you need to move past childish distractions and—dare I? Common *pleasures*, to put it nicely, and claim your rightful position in this world."

Common... Anger flared in Amery, incensing him. There was nothing *common* about how he felt for Tovin, or the knight's love in return. Pulling free from Bellona's grasp, Amery glared at her. "Advisor or not," he spat, "you speak out of turn, madam. I shall take the crown when I feel I am ready—or I may abdicate, again, when I must. Not when you think I should."

One jeweled hand reached out to smooth down the front of his coverlet with a mother's touch, straightening his buttons. "A knight is not worthy of a king's love," Bellona murmured. Amery shoved her hand away, but it drifted to his collar instead, straightening it. "He is a commoner, Your Highness. An admirable fighter, to be sure, but a soldier nonetheless. Nothing more than a pawn to be played in this game of war. A proper king needs a queen by his side, a lady of regal bearing, one with royal blood. Women love in ways with which a man could never compete."

If all women were as wily and manipulative as Bellona, Amery would never allow such a viper into his heart. "Your advice is just that," he told her, moving out of reach. "Words, my lady, and nothing more. Good day."

Before she could reply, he turned away. But he only took a few steps before another thought struck and he stopped. With a glance over his shoulder at Bellona, he told her, "And you know *nothing* about the man beneath the armor, I assure you."

Her eyes widened, but he didn't think his admission came as a surprise. She herself had brought Tovin up, which meant she knew of the regent's indiscretion. *Which is why she's pressuring me to take the crown—so I will be forced to leave him behind.*

I'll not do it.

Amery's heels rang off the stone floor as he set a furious pace down the hall. The black mood that had been hanging over him returned, no longer merely a pretense maintained for the servants' sake.

INSIDE THE WAR room, Tovin stood behind a long, low table covered with maps. A young squire leaned beside him—when Amery entered the room, his hands clenched into fists when he saw the squire, the same boy Berik had flirted with the night before. He stood too close to Tovin, as if hoping the knight would look up from his work to notice him. Too damn close…the look in his eyes was dulled with lust, and as Amery watched, the squire's tongue darted out to lick his lips, and one hand drifted to his crotch to rub obscenely at the bulge already straining his breeches.

"You," Amery spat. Both Tovin and the squire jumped at the regent's voice. When Tovin noticed the squire so close, he took a step away, distancing himself. Pointing at the empty corridor behind him, Amery ordered, "Out."

The squire frowned, confusion marring his young features. He glanced at Tovin, as if the knight might somehow intercede on his behalf, but Tovin ignored him and watched Amery instead. The boy's hesitation only fueled the rage warring inside Amery. "Are you deaf?" he snapped. "Get out. If I have to ask again, you will hang for such disrespect."

Quickly, the squire gathered up a handful of maps, sputtering apologies. "I am sorry, Your Highness," he said with a deep bow that dropped half his scrolls to the floor. "Your presence startled me—"

"He has that effect on people," Tovin drawled.

Amery saw the corner of his lover's mouth twitch in an effort not to grin. Keeping his voice stern, he warned, "I shall deal with you next. Once this miserable pimple is out of my sight. Why have you not yet left, squire?"

"I…I'm trying." The squire squatted on the floor, scrambling with maps that refused to stay put in his trembling hands. "I shall see to it the guards get these, Sir Tovin. If you need me for anything further—"

Amery sighed, exasperated. "He won't, trust me. Leave the maps where they lie and leave my sight *immediately*. Or you *will* be flogged!"

Crablike, the squire scuttled through the doorway and disappeared down the hall. Amery slammed the door shut behind him, throwing the bolt for added measure. As he kicked his way through the maps littering the floor, the amusement sparkling like dew in Tovin's eyes only made him frown harder.

"Your Highness," the knight purred, his tone of voice much more soothing than Bellona's had been. When Amery was close enough, the knight reached out to take his hand and pulled him near. "To what do I owe this honor?"

Amery wasn't ready to be placated yet. "He was all over you," he fumed. "How could you not notice—"

"Because I only see you." Curving his forefinger beneath Amery's chin, he raised the regent's face toward his for a sweet, lingering kiss. "You're just a jealous man, seeing things that aren't there."

Tovin's arms held him tight. "Of course I'm jealous." He picked at a stray thread in his lover's surcoat and struggled to rein in emotions that exhausted him. "That…that *squire* does what he likes with whomever catches his fancy. Last night he flirted with Berik at my table, *shameless*. And today he's here with you, fondling himself as he entertains who knows what sort of wicked thoughts…"

A smirk tugged at Tovin's mouth. "If he spent the night with Berik," he teased gently, "perhaps what you mistook for arousal was nothing more than a deep, burning *itch*."

Amery pulled out of his lover's embrace and leaned against the table, crossing his arms, sullen. "Regardless, I am a prisoner in this castle, Tovin. You know it. The crown dangles above me like the hangman's noose. My advisers pressure me into taking it, and now Bellona has the *audacity* to tell me that bedding a knight does not befit my stature. As if I have no say in the matter of who I am to love."

"Ah." Tovin turned back to his maps, the smile on his face soured. "So that's what this is all about. Beautiful *Bellona*. If witchcraft were a crime, she'd be the first to burn."

With a laugh, Amery sidled up behind him and wrapped his arms around his lover's waist. Kissing the knight's exposed neck, he murmured, "Can't we stop these war games now? Put away our crowns and our swords? I want you."

"I'm in the middle of something," Tovin replied, but he laced his fingers through Amery's and leaned back into his embrace. "I'll be finished shortly."

Amery sighed. "When?" Before Tovin could reply, he added, "You've been poring over those maps all day long.

You're neglecting me."

With a sardonic glance over his shoulder, Tovin said, "I am not neglecting you."

For the first time all day, Amery grinned. "You *are*." Skirting around Tovin, he eased between the knight and the table. Tovin gave ground without comment, leaning against Amery as the regent glanced at the map the knight had been studying. Even in this position, Amery loved the way their bodies fit together. Ignoring the start of an erection that prodded his buttocks, Amery pointed at the top map. "What's this?"

Tovin hugged Amery close and buried his nose in the regent's hair. "The castle floor plans," he explained. "I'm trying to get a handle on the layout of this place. If I am to protect it—"

"Where's my room?" Amery interrupted. He spotted a large area that filled one section of the map and pointed to it. "Is this it? My chambers?"

But Tovin laughed. "That's the ballroom, silly." Taking Amery's hand in his, he guided the regent's finger until it pointed to a small square in the far right corner. "That's your room."

"Looks smaller on paper." Amery flashed a wicked grin over his shoulder. "Let's go there now."

"Let me finish here," Tovin told him. "Then we can go."

Turning in Tovin's arms, Amery sighed. "But I want you *now*," he said, tugging at the knight's surcoat. "You just don't *know* the day I've had. I *need* you—"

Without warning, Tovin pushed the maps aside and hoisted Amery up onto the table. Amery wrapped his legs around Tovin's waist and pulled him closer, the knight's hands strong on his hips and back, his mouth pressed hungrily against Amery's own. Cradling Tovin's face in both hands, Amery moaned into their kisses, and when Tovin cupped his buttocks, raising him off the table, the regent thrust against his lover, legs tightening around Tovin's waist. "I want you," Amery sighed as Tovin leaned him back onto the table. With a suggestive tug at the knight's surcoat, he asked, "Right here?"

"No," Tovin replied with a smile. "I've got work to do." He grabbed the closest map and spread it out across Amery's body, once again engrossed in the castle floor plans.

Amery pushed the top of the map down off his face. "Tovin!" he cried. "I thought—"

"I know what you thought," Tovin said, poking at the map where it covered Amery's crotch. "Just give me a little bit longer, okay?"

"No," Amery said, sitting up. He shoved the map aside and slid off the table. "It is *not* okay. You'll not play with me like this."

Tovin gave him an innocent smile. "But it's so much fun. Do you know how cute you are when you're infuriated?"

Before Amery could answer, Tovin kissed him, a quick, soft touch that left the regent hungry for more. "Give me a quarter of an hour," the knight whispered. "Then I'm yours for the rest of the night."

Amery sighed again. "Promise?"

"Promise," Tovin replied. As Amery moved away from the table, Tovin gave his butt a playful slap. "I love you."

"I know," Amery said loftily. He grinned at the hurt look on Tovin's face. "See? It's not so fun when you're the one being played, is it?"

"Come here," Tovin growled, catching Amery's hand in his. He pulled the regent back and kissed his cheek. "Stop being a royal pain."

"I am not," Amery started, but Tovin quieted him with another kiss.

CHAPTER 7

WHEN TOVIN MANAGED to extract himself from his duties, more than a quarter of an hour had passed. Once the regent had left, the squire returned, and Tovin was careful to keep the table between them at all times. Still, minutes rushed by, tumbling into hours, and it wasn't until he heard the evening prayer bells ring from the chapel's tower that he realized how late it had grown. "Shit," he muttered, rolling up the nearest map. To the squire, he ordered, "See to it that these are put away. I am late for an audience with the regent."

Very late. Given Amery's earlier mood, Tovin suspected he would have a *lot* of making up to do.

The door to the regent's chambers was locked. Tovin did not expect that—he had one hand on the knob and walked right into the oaken door. A snicker escaped one of the guards stationed nearby, but when Tovin glared at them, they found something much more interesting to study on the floor or ceiling and refused to meet his gaze. Raising one hand curled into a fist, he pounded the door and ignored the hot stares on his back.

When he had to knock a second time, Tovin felt his own irritation begin to rise. In a commanding voice, he hollered, "Do not make me break down this door, Your Highness!"

He heard the scramble of locks, then the door opened an inch. Amery's young page peered out and blanched when he saw Tovin blocking the way. "Sir Tovin," he stuttered, bowing low while trying to hold the door shut. He simply succeeded in bumping his forehead against the door jamb. Rubbing the tender spot, he looked past Tovin to the guards and mumbled, "The regent is busy at the moment—"

"He will see me." Tovin shoved the door open, easily moving the page aside. As he entered the regent's sitting room, Tovin took in the empty chaise lounge, the low fire smoldering in the hearth, the dim lighting. Through the doorway into the other room, he saw the bed neatly made; there was no sign of Amery. Rounding on the page, he barked, "I have urgent matters to discuss with him. Where the hell is he?"

The page closed the door, then leaned back against it as if he were afraid Tovin might attack him out of spite. "The bath, sir. He said no one was to disturb him."

With a laugh, Tovin helped himself to the carafe of wine set out on a nearby credenza. Pouring a goblet, he sniffed at the blood-red liquid, then sipped the tepid wine. It seemed to suck all the moisture from his mouth, it was that dry. "Announce my presence," he told the page, when it became obvious the boy did not plan to move. "Tell the regent to stop whatever *solitary* pleasures in which he may be indulging at the moment. I will not wait long for him to come."

His double entendre was lost on the boy, who opened his mouth to speak, thought better of it, then hurried from the sitting room. The bath was a large basin set in the floor off Amery's bedroom—Tovin drifted to the doorway to listen in as the page approached the regent. He stared into the flickering flames in the hearth and from the other room, Amery's waspish voice snapped, "Who was it? I hope you sent them away."

Tovin didn't hear the page's reply, but Amery shouted,

"Why didn't you *say* so?"

The knight grinned at the splash of water on stone and could imagine all too well the glorious sight of his lover standing in the bath, water and soap running down the flat plains of his body. He'd snatch a robe, maybe wrap a towel around his long hair, and rush out to see what Tovin wanted. His skin would be clean and fragrant, warm beneath the absorbent robe, still slightly damp…

But it wasn't Amery who stepped through the doorway into the sitting room; it was his page. Tovin set his goblet on the mantle above the hearth, face hardening into the mask he wore around the servants. "Well?"

With a low bow, the page admitted, "I have been dismissed for the rest of the evening. The regent asks that you ensure his chamber door is locked when I leave, and says you can find your own way to the bath. Any business you have with him tonight may be conducted there."

Tovin struggled against the foolish grin that wanted to split his face. With a nod, he indicated the same door the page had tried to block earlier. The boy took a step toward it, then turned back to the knight, indecision twisting his young features. In a small voice, he admitted, "I fear leaving the two of you alone. The way you fight…"

"I am the regent's knight," Tovin reminded him. He let slip a hint of a smile, and that seemed to relax the boy. "I assure you, despite our differences, he is safe with me."

"Yes, Sir Tovin." He nodded, then hurried from the room, closing the chamber door behind him.

Tovin waited, sipping his wine, until he heard an irritated splash from the bath. A few moments later, Amery called out, "Tovin?"

Moving quietly, Tovin crossed the sitting room and latched the door. Then he downed the rest of his wine; the alcohol warmed him like dragon's breath, curling down his throat and into his belly where it banked, waiting to burst into flame. As he headed for the doorway between the rooms, he began to strip—first his surcoat, which fell to the floor by the chaise lounge, then his scabbard clattered down beside it. Amery must have heard the noise, for he called out again, "Tovin? Isn't that damn page gone *yet?*"

Without answering, Tovin shucked off his boots, hopping from one foot to the other to remove them. Entering the bedroom, he untied his breeches, pushed them down, stepped out of them, then did the same with the bries he wore against his skin. Naked now, he padded barefoot to the elaborate folding screen that separated the bath from the rest of the room. He heard more water splashing, and Amery muttering beneath his breath. The regent was nothing if not impatient.

The thought made Tovin smile. Regardless, he loved that man.

At the last moment, he ducked down behind the screen. Keeping out of view, he snuck along its length, away from the opening where Amery would be expecting him to appear. Instead, Tovin entered the bath from the other side, easing into the slim gap between the screen and the wall.

The basin had been cut from the floor around it, large enough for a man to recline in comfortably. The sides were sloped, allowing the regent to lean back with his head propped on a small pillow outside the tub. Nothing looked more relaxing. Tovin often thought of the regent's bath when he was out in the field, scrubbing in streams or standing water in any attempt at cleanliness.

At the moment, soapy water lapped the edge of the tub, and puddles formed on the tiles where Amery had splashed it out. The pillow had fallen away, and Amery sat with his back to the knight as he ran a washcloth down one arm. All Tovin could see of the regent was the back of his head and shoulders—the rest was hidden by the suds in the tub. Amery's long hair had been piled into a loose knot onto the top of his head, and the heat from the water curled the few strands of hair that had escaped the bun to rest against his nape. Tovin approached on tiptoe, not quite sure what he'd do to get the regent's attention but looking forward to the moment his lover turned to see him…

Suddenly Amery cried out, "Tovin!" Anger laced his words. In a quieter voice, he muttered, "Where the fuck *are* you? No one *else* keeps me waiting."

Tovin suppressed a laugh, but when the regent stood from the tub, the vision that rose before the knight silenced him. Lust and desire crashed through him like surf as he saw Amery's freckled skin slicked with water, suds sluiced away over taut flesh. When the regent moved toward the far edge of the bath to exit the tub, Tovin seized the opportunity to slip into the water immediately behind his lover.

The water was much hotter than it looked—the moment Tovin stepped into it, he felt a deep flush rise up his legs and sweat beaded his brow. With a gasp, he pressed his dry body to Amery's wet skin; they molded together perfectly, like stitches interlaced in an elaborate tapestry. His arms snaked around the regent's wet hips, his hands already reaching for the length that hung between Amery's legs. Hugging his lover close, Tovin nosed aside the stray hairs on Amery's neck to kiss the pinked, warm skin behind his ear. One hand found the regent's cock, already erect. "Pleasuring yourself?" Tovin whispered. "Your Highness, why was I not invited?"

"You were," Amery countered, leaning back against the knight, "hours ago."

Tovin's reply was a suckling kiss that left a damp imprint of his lips on the regent's shoulder. One hand smoothed up Amery's chest, trailing over wet skin, as he massaged his lover's balls with the other. His own dick pressed between Amery's buttocks as if eager for entry. "Are you clean yet?" the knight teased. "Because your bed awaits."

Amery turned in Tovin's embrace but only managed a brief kiss before he lost his footing in the tub and slipped. His lips glanced across Tovin's one moment; the next he sat at Tovin's feet, a surge of water slapping along the tiled floor. The look on his face was something between mirth and pain, like a child who has fallen and isn't quite sure whether to laugh or cry. Dropping to his knees in the bathwater, Tovin reached for his lover, concerned. "Are you all right, Amery?"

The regent took a deep breath, which escaped him in heady laughter. Tovin smacked the water, splashing them both. "You must be more *careful*," he admonished. "You are the regent—"

"I can fall on my ass if I want," Amery replied.

Beneath the water, his legs stretched out, one on either side of Tovin's knees. Leaning forward, the regent wrapped his arms around his lover's waist; the feel of skin on skin underwater made the most ordinary touch unfamiliar, exciting. Tovin allowed himself to be drawn nearer, and when he leaned Amery back against the side of the tub, he pulled the pin that held the regent's hair in place. Long auburn locks fell like curtains to frame Amery's face.

"Love me," Amery commanded. His hand found Tovin's cock under the water, his fingers kneading, tugging, working it erect. "I'll not be kept waiting. I want you."

Grabbing one of Amery's knees, Tovin propped it on his hip to open a space between his lover's legs. Then he moved closer, leaning down over his lover, letting Amery guide him where he wanted him. The other leg twined with Tovin's beneath the water, and their bodies slid together like two pieces of interlocking clockwork. Tovin's mouth covered Amery's as the tip of his dick pressed at the small, puckered hole at the regent's center.

With one hard thrust and a silencing kiss to counter Amery's discomfort, he entered him.

The regent's hands clawed at Tovin's back, fisted in his hair. The knight had to hold himself up against the bottom of the tub to keep from crushing Amery into the porcelain, and he moved slowly, feeling his cock fill his lover, feeling the water move around them with their rhythm. The heat from the water made them both blush. Tovin felt the night stretch out around them, full of possibility, full of love.

But after a few languid thrusts, Amery wanted more. He took control of their lovemaking, sliding out from under Tovin while holding the knight close, both with his arms and the muscles of his ass, keeping him in as he repositioned them. Now *he* was on top, and Tovin found himself laying back against the side of the tub, the regent pierced on his throbbing cock. As he rode Tovin, Amery sat up in the water, gripping the sides of the tub—the ends of his hair were dark red and wet, and water dripped down his chest. "Yes," he cried, rocking above Tovin. His voice rang from the tiles and off the stone walls. "Yes, harder, *yes, yes!*"

Tovin held Amery's hips as he fucked into him. The regent released the sides of the tub to finger Tovin's nipples, but the touch excited the knight too much—he slid down into the water to keep Amery from picking at them. It wouldn't do to come too soon and lose this moment. Amery bucked above him, riding him, then reached out and stretched down over Tovin to grasp the sides of the tub behind the knight's head. With wild abandon, the regent moved above his knight, straddling him, loving him, faster, harder, *deeper* as they rushed to release.

Water splashed from the tub, its steady *slap slap slap* matching their furious pace. Tovin kissed Amery's chest, his throat, the thinly muscled arms stretched on either side of his head. His cock moved through the hot water, driving into his lover's tight ass, bringing them both to the edge of orgasm.

Just before he climaxed, Tovin slid into the water. It closed over the top of his head, washing away the sweat and grime on his face. The world thundered around him unseen, sounds distorted, touch unreal. Amery's hands reached for him, found the hard buds of his nipples, and tweaked as the regent pressed him to the bottom of the tub. He sat heavily on Tovin's cock, his body pinning him down, and Tovin could feel the regent's shuddering heartbeat pulse against the tip of his dick, so deep inside his lover. The slightest movement sent waves of pleasure roiling through him, through them both. The sensation built up between them, rising to a crescendo, rising in pitch like the steam in a teapot, until it shattered beneath his lover's distant touch. The rush of jism from his cock matched the roar of water in his ears and the pounding blood in his veins. A double heartbeat pulsed through the water, two men made one by a single love.

Then Amery pulled him from the bath. As he broke the surface of the water, Tovin gasped for breath and found his lover's mouth on his in a resurrecting kiss.

CHAPTER 8

WHEN THE WATER began to cool, they climbed out of the tub. Tovin first—he grabbed one of the towels that hung over the top of the screen and held it open, enveloping Amery as the regent stepped up to him. Another towel he used to dry himself with rough, fast motions while Amery sat on the page's chair beside the screen, huddled in his towel, waiting. Finally as dry as he was likely to get, Tovin replaced his towel with a thick robe. The regent's robe had his crest on the left breast; this larger robe had once belonged to the king, but Amery had long since nicked it from his father's chamber for Tovin's use.

Taking Amery's teal robe from where it hung on the corner of the screen, Tovin draped it over his lover's shoulders and rubbed some warmth into the wet skin. "Put this on or you'll get sick," he instructed. The castle was too drafty to parade around after a bath, and the bedroom's fire muttered low in the hearth, barely warming the room.

Without a word, Amery complied. He snaked his arms into the robe, then drew it closed around him, over the towel. Squatting beside his chair, Tovin took one of Amery's feet in both his hands and rubbed it dry with his own towel. His hands were gentle, his touch loving, his fingers massaging as he wiped between each toe and around the sole of Amery's foot, then around his ankle, then up his leg to his knee. When he was finished with the first leg, he moved to the other. He was halfway up Amery's left calf when he heard a muffled sob above him.

He looked up to find Amery's robe pulled to hide his face. Though he couldn't begin to understand what might be bothering his lover, Tovin dropped the towel and took the regent into his arms. "It's all right," he murmured, smoothing his hand along Amery's warm back. "Shh, love. It's not so bad."

"I *hate* this," Amery spat.

Tovin knew he didn't mean this tender moment between them—the regent hiccupped, trying to compose himself, but only seemed to cry harder. He clung to Tovin with a desperation that scared the knight. "It's grown late, Your Highness." Tovin hugged him close, as if that would help stem his tears. "Tomorrow will be a better day."

Sniffling, Amery wiped his eyes on Tovin's shoulder and sighed. "I'll not take the crown," he announced. His fists clenched in Tovin's robe, keeping him near. "Not if I must lose you in the bargain. I cannot do it."

Tovin grinned. "You can't live without me," he teased. "I know."

But Amery didn't find that humorous. "I can't." He sat back just enough to allow him to stare into Tovin's eyes; his gaze was earnest, enhanced by his tear-streaked cheeks. "I will not take that crown."

Weariness filled Tovin—he didn't *want* Amery to take it, if he were being honest, but that was selfish of him and he had long ago promised himself that when the time came, he would support whichever decision his lover made. The people needed a king, the *land* needed one, more than either of them needed to be happy. Tovin would protect Amery to the death, whether or not he slept with the man. In a perfect world, he'd love the regent regardless of the crown.

But the world beyond the regent's chamber was far from perfect.

Gently, Tovin pointed out, "You're made for the crown, Amery. You *are* the regent, you say it often enough yourself. Eventually you *must* take it."

"I'll die." Amery shook his head, flinging the hair from his face. "I shall kill myself before I wear it. With your blade if I must."

Tovin saw something wicked flash in his lover's eyes, a gleam that seemed to like that suggestion. With a sigh, the knight pointed out, "Then your court will think I did it. They believe we hate each other as it is. If you die by my blade, I will hang a murderer."

Amery fell silent. His eyes dulled, and a slight pout tugged at his lips. Then another thought struck him, and he grasped Tovin's hand in both of his. "I shall write a note—"

"Most of your servants cannot read," Tovin pointed out. He wanted to laugh at the crestfallen look on the regent's face, but tamped down the urge, waiting to see what his lover came up with next.

"I shall have someone with me," Amery muttered, half to himself. "Bellona, perhaps…"

Now Tovin *did* laugh. "She'd plunge the blade into your heart for you, and twist it out of spite."

Amery shook his head, discounting her. "My page, then."

"And terrorize the boy?" Tovin joked. "Surely he's much too young. He'll be rendered speechless by the shock of it, unable to tell a soul."

The regent punched his shoulder in anger. "Stop shooting down my ideas, Tovin. I will *not* take that crown."

"What about me?" the knight asked. When Amery looked at him, Tovin gave him a sad, exaggerated pout. "What would happen to me if you died? How would *I* go on?"

After a moment's hesitation, Amery told him, "Well, I

would hope you'd never take another lover. In fact, I forbid it."

"You'll be gone," Tovin countered. "Who'll stop me?"

Exasperated, Amery cried, "Tovin! I'm trying to be serious here."

Rising to his feet, the knight ran an arm beneath the regent's legs, the other behind his back, and swooped him into his arms. Amery clutched at Tovin's robe and laughed, a boyish sound that dispersed their gloomy discussion. "Remember when I cut my leg that time?" he asked, holding onto Tovin tightly as the knight carried him to the bed. "How old was I, like twelve?"

"Eleven." Tovin remembered the moment with perfect clarity—the five of them had been playing by the moat, racing across the open drawbridge with a thundering noise only teenage boys could make. Amery tripped on the bolt that held the rusty metal chain to the bridge, and when he regained his footing, the right leg of his breeches had been dark with blood.

Tovin reacted before the others even realized something had happened. Without a thought, he scooped the prince into his arms and raced across the bridge, holding Amery close. Spurred into action, their friends flew past them, into the castle, calling for a physician. To this day he could still recall how Amery had felt in his arms, so frail, like a wounded bird; he could remember the boy's grimy scent, the stuttering heartbeat against his, the hand that pulled at his hair in an effort to hold on.

Crown or no, Tovin would *not* lose those memories, or this man. He *couldn't*.

Lowering Amery onto the bed, Tovin lay down beside him. Amery's head rested on Tovin's chest, and he opened the robe a bit to press his lips against the knight's neck. "I don't want this to end," he whispered. "Not ever."

Tovin smiled as he kissed Amery's temple. "You're the regent," he replied. "Isn't your word law?"

"You mock me," Amery sighed.

"I try," Tovin purred. His next kiss landed on Amery's

cheek. "Pretend for a moment you don't take the crown—"

Amery interrupted him. "I won't! I refuse."

Tovin kissed him quiet. "Listen. If you don't, where would you go?"

There was no hesitation in the regent's voice. "With you."

"I would have to leave the military," Tovin admitted. The thought bothered him, but not as much as he once believed it would. Until this moment in time, he had never realized it, but a part of him must've known all along that his livelihood as a knight would have to be discarded if Amery abdicated. Funny how he found that he had a plan already on the tip of his tongue, ready to share. Laying back against the downy comforter, he hugged Amery close and wove a dream for the two of them. "In the southland, my sister owns an inn. Just outside Konstas. For years she's been trying to sell the place, but no one has taken her up on the offer."

Seizing the dream, Amery suggested, "I could buy it. Now, or tomorrow, rather. I'll dispatch a courier to sign the deed."

Tovin grinned. "I'm just talking out loud here," he murmured. "Tomorrow you'll have a good night's sleep behind you, and you'll forget all about giving up the crown."

"No." Amery tried to sit up but Tovin held him down, so he settled for turning his face up to search his lover's. Lowering his voice, he promised, "I'll not lose you. There is nothing in this kingdom worth that price."

Tovin rested his forehead against Amery's and stared into his lover's eyes for a long moment, gauging the man he saw inside. He could tell by the determined set of the regent's jaw that he would never be crowned. But theirs was a forbidden love, and he knew many would not allow it to continue much longer. If Bellona suspected their relationship enough to voice concerns to the regent himself, then Tovin knew the royal adviser would soon take matters into her own hands to get what she wanted.

And, like the rest of Pharr, what she wanted was a king. A

mere knight like himself could hardly stand in her way.

Tovin nuzzled closer and pressed his lips against Amery's ear, whispering, "If anything should happen to me—"

"Like what?" Amery pulled away and frowned, his hands touching Tovin's face. "Nothing will happen to you. I won't let it."

Tovin kissed Amery's fingertips and sighed. "If it does," he tried again.

But Amery interrupted him. "Like what?" he demanded. "Tell me, Tovin. If what happens? You're stationed here, leagues from the northern border. There is nothing to harm you here."

With a shrug, Tovin hugged Amery to him again. "Not just that," he replied. "If there's a siege maybe, or a rebellion, or I don't know, anything at all. Someone killing me to force you to take the crown—"

Amery gasped in shock. "They *wouldn't.*"

"You don't know," Tovin told him. When Amery tried to pull away a second time, Tovin held him tight. "*Listen* to me. If anything should happen, to *either* of us—"

"It won't," Amery said, stubborn. His hair tickled Tovin's chest as he shook his head.

Tovin sighed. "If it *does,*" he said, and when Amery tried to argue, he covered his lover's mouth with his hand. "There isn't much time before you will have to choose and you know it. I am the only thing that stands between you and the throne. Eliminate me and your choice is clear."

Amery shook his head furiously, but Tovin kept his hand over his lover's mouth, silencing him. "If you still refuse the crown, your damned advisers will probably kill you, too, just out of spite. Bellona would, at least. So don't let them corner you. I will protect you as much as I can, Amery, I swear it. And if we're meant to be together, I know something will come up, some way will present itself. It *has* to."

Beneath his hand, Amery nodded. Kissing his ear, Tovin lowered his voice to mere breath as he sighed into his lover, "If something happens—to me, to the castle, anything at all that puts you in danger—I want you to run. Do you understand me? Don't stand and fight. There's a sluiceway that runs beneath the castle—" Amery licked Tovin's palm in an effort to get him to remove his hand, but Tovin simply laughed at the gesture. "Stop it and listen."

"I am listening," came the muffled reply.

Amery's eyes were shiny and large above Tovin's hand; the knight pressed his lips to his lover's ear again. "Stacia's is the last inn when you ride through Konstas. Two days' journey from here with a fast steed." He waited for Amery to nod before he continued. "There is no need to buy the place—I know my sister, and much as she complains about that inn, part of the reason she's had no buyers is that she refuses to sell. But she knows of us. If you ever find yourself free from the castle, go there. She will see to it you're kept safe until I can find you. Do you hear me?"

"Yes," Amery replied as Tovin removed his hand. "But nothing *will* happen."

"Perhaps not," Tovin said, snuggling closer to his lover. "But if it does, you run. Don't be contrary, just this once, please? Go to Stacia's, and when I can get away, I shall find you there."

"Okay," Amery whispered. With a grin, he added, "Just this once."

⚜

THE NEXT MORNING, Amery stretched himself awake. Fading dreams blurred his mind, lingering images of Tovin in him, loving him, holding him tight. But when he reached an arm out for his lover, he frowned to find the bed beside him empty. "Tovin?" he called. It wasn't *too* late in the day. The knight should still be in his chambers…

"I'm right here," Tovin assured him. His voice carried in from the sitting room, and as Amery settled back against the pillows, his lover came to stand in the doorway between the rooms. His breeches were already tied into place around his waist, and his heavy boots echoed off the stone floor with each step. As he shrugged on his surcoat, he winked at Amery. "Morning, glory. You looking for me?"

"Come here," Amery said, patting the blankets. "I command it."

Tovin laughed at that. "You command it?"

Amery sighed. There was a playful banter in his lover's voice that told him no amount of cajoling would get Tovin back between his sheets. With a pout, Amery tried, "Tovin…"

"I wasn't made castellan to spend my days in your bed. There's a war to be fought," the knight reminded the regent. "No amount of pretty pouting will turn the Cyrians around."

"Are you sure?" Amery teased. "Maybe if I ask real nice—"

"No," Tovin replied. Crossing the room, he leaned down to give Amery a quick peck on the cheek. When the regent turned, trying to catch that kiss on his lips instead, the knight pulled away. "There is work to be done, Your Highness. I have a castle to defend. Get your royal ass out of bed."

With another sigh, Amery kicked the sheets away. The knight's eyes widened at the sight of so much taut, nude flesh, and Amery allowed himself another languid stretch so his lover could see just what he was missing by not returning to the bed.

But Tovin was a stronger man than Amery—despite his greedy stare, he restrained himself. Only a faint tremor in his fingers as they buttoned his surcoat belayed his desire. As Amery lay amid his blankets, displaying his nude body for his lover, Tovin sighed. "What a glorious sight. Too bad I must get to work. Tonight—"

"I have to wait *that* long?" Amery cried.

With a laugh, Tovin turned and headed back into the sitting room. Amery climbed off the bed and, naked, followed the knight. When Tovin retrieved his sword from where it lay on the floor, Amery took it from him. "Let me," he said, securing the knight's sheath to his waist. "You're so dashing in armor."

"That won't get me back into the bedroom," Tovin warned.

Amery laughed. "I know. Your duty calls. Duty which *I* assigned." He kissed Tovin hungrily once, twice, and the third time the knight staggered back against the door beneath the regent's insistent attentions. "Tonight," Amery promised.

"Until then," Tovin agreed. His last kiss lingered on the regent's lips long after the chamber door closed behind him.

CHAPTER 9

TOVIN HAD A million things to do before he would consider the castle safe from attack—there were fortifications to check, ramparts to secure, a weak guard to whip back into shape…

And you shall think of the regent throughout the day.

Absently, he touched his hand to his face, where he could still feel the ghost of Amery's mouth against his. Whenever he closed his eyes, he saw Amery stretched out on his bed, his lithe, nude body begging for Tovin's touch. The evening when they could be alone again would not come soon enough.

He had been tempted to take Amery up on his offer—just spend the day in his lover's arms and let the others worry about the war that rumbled like a thundering cloud on their northern borders. Berik and Lohden would take care of the Cyrians, he knew it, and Giles's men would have no trouble stifling the few who dared to come into the kingdom from the west. Couriers had been dispatched the previous day, racing for the southland with news that would bring Tovin's own troops storming to the castle. Within three days at the most, his own men would fill these empty corridors, weapons at the ready. Nothing could bring down these stone walls, *nothing*.

Tovin would see to that.

But until he had those extra men under his command, he would stay wary. As they had cuddled in the regent's bed the night before, Tovin had gone over directions on how to get to the abandoned sluiceway that ran beneath the castle. He repeated them, over and over, forced the regent to repeat them as well, until they both felt comfortable about the plan. Now if an opportunity would just present itself...

The sluiceway was naught but an ancient piece of masonry, one they'd played in as children, one even he had forgotten about until he found it again while studying the castle maps. It ran straight beneath the garden where he'd first met the young prince, all those years ago. It was in that same garden where they'd first shared an experimental kiss, the beginning of a lifetime of kisses, when Amery had been a young boy barely fifteen years of age, a scrap of the man he'd become, but already beautiful in Tovin's eyes.

Despite the passage of time, the knight could still remember the nervousness that had churned his own stomach, and the way the regent's hands had twisted in his tunic. They'd huddled together in the shade of an old birch tree, out of sight from the castle. After the brief crush of their lips, Amery had sighed and flashed Tovin an anxious smile. "You taste sweet. I bet you hear that all the time."

"You're my first," Tovin admitted.

Amery's eyes went wide. "No. You're so much older than me."

Tovin laughed. "Who else do you think I've bothered to kiss? Lohden? *Giles?*"

Laughing himself, Amery suggested, "Berik."

But Tovin waved that away. "He's too damn hairy for me. I like you."

"I like you, too." Amery smiled again and scooted closer so he could rest his head on Tovin's shoulder. Picking at the knight's tunic, the prince whispered, "I think...I might like you more. I mean, I know I'm still too young, really, but maybe, if you don't have anyone else, and you don't mind much, maybe you'd want to be mine?"

Tovin felt his insides melt and he'd kissed Amery again. "There's no maybe about it."

On that day they became something more than friends. And three years later, when Amery turned of age, they became lovers in every sense of the word. Eight years had passed and still Tovin felt every ounce of affection the regent roused in him—over time, those boyish feelings had deepened into a love that burned in him like a small sun, shining over everything he said or did or thought, every aspect of his life.

He was glad Amery had promoted him to castellan; he would trust no one else with the duty of protecting the regent's life because none could ever feel as much for the man as he did himself. Tovin knew he alone would ensure the regent's safety, at any cost. *I'll not let them take him from me.*

He meant the Cyrians, but part of him meant the kingdom of Pharr, as well. He couldn't lose the one man he loved more than life itself. He *wouldn't*. He would give up his sword before he gave up Amery.

＋

FROM THE PARAPETS that crowned the castle's towers, Tovin could survey the land stretching away to the south of the castle. Forests bordered the keep to the north and east, a fact that Tovin didn't much like, but he didn't have the manpower at the moment to waste in clearing the trees. Once this threat was dispersed, he promised himself, frowning at the dark shadows that clung to the woods, he would have that forest pushed back about a league or so, just enough to give him any warning of an attack. In the meantime, he would simply have to tighten security on the northern wall.

As dusk began to fall, sputtering torches flared to life around the parapets. Tovin waited until the sun had dipped below the horizon and the whole castle was lit before satisfied he had done all he could for the evening. What few men were stationed at the castle as the regent's personal guards had been reassigned—they now dotted the parapets with arrows and buckets of oil, guarding the castle itself. They were a lax bunch, used to the comfortable life, but they snapped to attention when Tovin passed their posts and that was all he could ask. Earlier in the day, a runner had come from the south, announcing that Tovin's own men were already mounted and heading his way. If they rode through the night, as he suspected they would, then the castle could be fortified by their presence before noon the next day. That thought alone would allow Tovin to sleep well.

Retreating inside, he made his way to the regent's chambers with a thoughtful expression on his face. The runner bothered him; if the courier had managed to meet with Tovin's troops in record time, why had they had no word from Berik, Lohden, or Giles? Surely the three knights had reached their own troops already.

At the back of his mind, something else nagged at him, something just out of reach. He ran through the ramparts again, recalling the lay of the land surrounding the castle. The flat plains to the south, the rolling hills west, the cluster of trees and shade that festered to the east and north like a dark, seeping wound. Something bothered him about those forests, something he couldn't quite place...

You're just being overly cautious.

True. He reached Amery's chamber door and raised his hand to knock, but dropped it to the knob instead. It turned easily beneath his hand, but he wasn't ready to let the worry fall from him just yet. In the morning he would ride out there himself, he decided. *I'll survey the trees and maybe start clearing them away. I won't accomplish much, but it will ease my mind, at least.*

Yes, he'd do that. In the morning, when there was light to see by, he'd ride a little way into the trees, just to put his fear to rest. As he opened the regent's door, he smiled at the thought that maybe Amery would ride with him. Just the two of them, alone in the woods, free from the constant supervision of the servants and the guard…free to linger in the shadows, or make love on the moss-covered ground…

"There you are," Amery purred.

Locking the door behind him, Tovin turned to find Amery stretched out on the chaise lounge in his sitting room. Still nude, as if he had not bothered to dress the entire day, he lay with one arm draped over the back of the chaise lounge and his legs parted in invitation. He looked as if he had not moved since Tovin left him that morning.

He was gorgeous.

Tovin took in the vision of his lover's freckled skin, naked and smooth and dappled with a golden glow cast by the fire. His long auburn hair had been pulled back in a loose braid, and his pale eyes danced with firelight. In front of the chaise lounge, a small table was set, laden with fresh berries and slivers of rich cake.

The regent's cock was already rigid with desire; it pointed up at his navel, hard against his lower belly, and one hand toyed with the foreskin, sliding it back and forth, allowing the damp tip to peek out, then disappear again. Leaning back against the chaise lounge, Amery sighed. "I've been waiting forever."

Tovin's sword landed on the floor with a clank, his mail following suit. In two steps he was leaning over his lover, pressing Amery back against the chaise lounge as he kissed him hungrily. His hand strayed to his lover's crotch, where it cupped the soft sac of the regent's balls. "Forever?" he murmured against Amery's lips. "You poor boy."

"I know," Amery conceded.

Nimbly, he untethered Tovin's shirt, his fingers finding pinked nipples and teasing them erect. Tovin gasped with delight at the shivers that ran through him at that touch. In his breeches, his dick went from mildly aroused to rock solid in the time it took his lover to make his nipples stand beneath his fingers. Amery's mouth was hot on his, ardent, his tongue licking into him as if staking claim.

Tovin's hand smoothed along his lover's muscular chest, slipping across his flat stomach and lower, until his fingers twisted in kinked hair and Amery thrust into his closed fist. "Please…"

"The regent begs," Tovin teased, and the frustration that crossed Amery's face made the rest of the world disappear. "Tell me you want me."

Amery pouted. "You know I do," he whispered, helping Tovin out of his shirt. Tossing the garment to the floor, he said, "Kiss me again."

"You aren't playing along." Tovin squeezed his lover's erection. "Tell me you want me."

"I do," Amery replied. "Please, Tovin. *Please*—"

Tovin sighed. "I guess that will suffice," he whispered against Amery's neck. "I give in too easily to you…you know that, right?"

Amery laughed and hugged Tovin to him. "It's because you love me."

"I do," Tovin admitted.

Amery managed to get the knight's breeches untied and pushed them down past his thighs, hands already kneading Tovin's weeping erection. When Tovin raised a knee to straddle Amery, his breeches threatened to tear at the seams, stretched across the chaise lounge and keeping the knight from opening his legs farther. Amery's hands encircled his shaft; his fingers were oiled, scented with perfume, and they slid along Tovin's hard cock with ease, massaging it, tugging at the swollen tip. Placing his hands on the back of the chaise lounge, one on either side of Amery's head, Tovin thrust into the regent's grip and moaned his lover's name.

Then the regent sat up, his tongue licking out to connect with Tovin's flesh, and when his teeth caught one tender nipple between them, Tovin couldn't help himself—the orgasm he tried so hard to hold back surged through him, and a dribble of cum squirted from his cockhead onto Amery's already slicked hands. With a breathless laugh, the knight admitted, "I don't think I can hold out against you much longer."

A knock on the chamber door interrupted them.

Tovin stopped in mid-thrust; Amery's teeth released his nipple and the regent leaned against the knight's chest to mutter, "Fuck."

Tovin laughed again, a shaky sound. As the pleasure in him receded, he reined in his lustful desire and managed to pull himself back from the edge of release. Kissing the top of his lover's head, he murmured into Amery's thick hair, "Tell them to go away."

Without moving, Amery raised his voice. "Go away, damn it! I told you I wanted to be alone tonight."

"You're not exactly *alone*," Tovin joked.

"That's beside the point," Amery told him. The knock sounded again; the regent shook his head, negating the sound. "I'll not answer it. The kingdom can fall for all I care—"

From the hallway they heard a rush of footsteps and then the page's voice called out, hollow through the thick door. "Your Highness, please! It's important."

"It better be," Amery grumbled.

Tovin stood and tugged up his breeches. As he tucked himself into the fabric, Amery surged to his feet and pushed past his lover, a look of pure hatred twisting his beautiful features. Scooping the knight's shirt from where it had fallen to the floor, Amery fisted it at his crotch, then threw open his chamber door to glare at the boy standing in the hall. "Well?" he asked hotly. "What the hell is it?"

"A rider," the boy answered. His gaze flickered down Amery's nude body to the shirt clenched at his crotch. His eyes widened slightly, his mouth a perfect O of surprise. Then he glanced past Amery to take in Tovin, shirtless, sitting on the edge of the chaise lounge and nibbling at a piece of cake. Ignoring the regent, the page said, "Sir Tovin, I came looking for you, actually."

Tovin stared at Amery's naked buttocks, clenched in his anger. Twin dimples marred the otherwise flawless skin. He imagined licking those dimples, smoothing that flesh out with his lips, nipping at it until it reddened beneath his teeth... "You found me."

"A rider from the north," the boy stammered, hurrying on. "He asks for you."

The north. So Berik *had* sent word. Tovin rose to his feet. "I shall see him."

"Tovin," Amery whined. He shut the door in the page's face as the knight belted his sword into place. "Can this not wait?"

"I shall be right back," Tovin promised. He kissed Amery, a quick peck on the corner of his mouth, and pulled his shirt out of the regent's hand. "I believe this is mine."

In the hallway he shrugged into the shirt, fastening it as he hurried after the page. The scent of Amery's oils rose from the fabric like a cloud enveloping him, a heady combination of patchouli and sage. It only incensed the ache in his crotch. He wanted nothing more than to turn around and take his lover in his arms, dive into the tight warmth at his center, and let his stymied orgasm loose. But duty first... "A rider, you say?"

The page nodded. "Sir Berik himself. He rode—"

"Sir Berik?" Tovin broke into a trot, forcing the boy to run ahead of him. "Why did you not say so? What's he doing here?" Berik was supposed to be commanding troops, not racing back to the castle. *Where's Lohden? What the hell is going on?*

Questions the page would be unable to answer. Aloud, Tovin asked, "When did he arrive?"

"Minutes ago." The page led the way through the castle halls. "He says it's urgent he sees you."

They rounded a corner and, as if his words had brought the man into being, right into Sir Berik. The page slammed into the knight, who caught him easily. "Tovin," Berik gasped, breathless. Pushing the boy aside, he lowered his voice and looked around, eyes wild in his bearded face. His ruddy cheeks were flushed a deep shade of red, like twin beets. "God."

"What is it?" Tovin demanded. He tucked his shirt into his pants and cursed the fact that he had left his mail lying on Amery's floor. "Berik? Talk to me. What are you doing back? And where's Lohden?"

"Dead." Berik leaned against the wall and gripped his head in both hands. "At least I think he is. We didn't see them coming. We didn't know until it was too late…"

"See who?" Tovin wanted to know. "Berik, the Cyrians? Where are they?"

His voice was barely a whisper when he replied, "In the woods."

The woods…

Berik continued. "They've surrounded the castle, Tovin. They were closer than we thought. *Much* closer. We stumbled upon their camp and I sent Lohden west to catch up with Giles while I raced back here but they were right behind me. We never even reached our men. I suspect they will attack at any moment now—"

"Battle stations!" Tovin roared.

His cry rang off the stone walls and startled a guard posted nearby. When the man frowned at him, Tovin pushed him into action. "I want men at every entrance," he commanded. The guard gave a curt nod. "Double the guard outside the regent's chambers, do you understand? He is not to leave his chambers. Tell the archers to concentrate on the forest. Douse the torches but spare a few to light the oil."

Another nod. Tovin shoved the guard down the hall. "Go!"

As the man raced from the corridor, Tovin took Berik's arm and tugged his friend after him. "Come on."

"Where are we going?" Berik asked.

"The ramparts," Tovin replied. He had a castle to defend.

CHAPTER 10

THE FIRST ATTACK came before they reached the parapets. Tovin heard the thunder of siege engines and then the stone around them shook as the machines unleashed their artillery on the castle walls. He staggered in the stairwell, Berik falling away behind him as another volley struck. *Keep Amery safe,* he prayed, pushing his way through the servants scrambling down the steps. *Please let him stay out of harm's way.*

At the parapets, Tovin looked down over the northern face of the castle and frowned at what he saw. The night below him was alive with bonfires, their shadows flickering in the light and the trees. He couldn't tell how large the army was, how many men he was up against, what weaponry they had...splashing in the moat told him their border had been breached, and as he stood there, assessing the situation, one of the courtyard walls was pulled to the ground. "This is no good," he muttered.

Berik laughed, a short, rough sound that scared him. "You wanted to fight," he reminded Tovin. "Here's your chance. They came knocking for you...shit."

But Tovin shook his head and leaned over the parapet, trying to stare into the battle roiling in the darkness beneath them. He had wanted a chance to fight the barbarians, yes—hordes of ruthless, lawless men rumored to eat their victims and drink the blood they spilled on the battlefield. But he never wanted to bring the war this close to the castle, to *Amery*. *I never meant to bring them here.*

With a shaky sigh, Berik glanced around at the men rushing by them, readying their defenses. "Is the regent—"

"Fine," Tovin replied quickly. Cheers rose from the western wing of the castle, where the Cyrians managed to break through the guard and were beginning to enter the courtyard, crawling over the crumbled walls like insects. It was only a matter of time before the whole place fell.

Tovin gripped the rough stone in both hands and fought the urge to race back to the regent's chambers. There were guards stationed at his door; they would protect him. They *had* to. Tovin was needed elsewhere. *Please*, he prayed, hoping his plea would be heard over the rising din of battle. *Please keep him safe.*

✦

AMERY FELT THE castle shake beneath a volley of cannon fire and knew Tovin would not be back. He dressed quickly, his heart in his throat, his dick no longer interested in lustful play. The rider must've been sent with news that the Cyrians were nearby, but this close? He had never imagined the threat to be *that* imminent. They had so few men guarding the castle…when would the knights' armies arrive? Could the castle hold fast that long?

Another booming attack shook the walls around him and he suspected he already knew the answer to *that* question. If the Cyrians forded the moat, if they had siege engines with them, if they had the element of surprise in their favor…then no, the castle would not last until dawn.

Tovin's voice rose in his mind, unbidden. *Off the servant's quarters, through the pantry, there is a small door along the back wall that opens into the sluiceway. It was once used to toss old food, to keep beggars from rooting through the King's garbage, but when the sewers were rebuilt, this one was abandoned. You have to get down on your hands and knees and crawl through…*

Amery shook the words away as he fastened his coverlet into place. The sluiceway was a dream, something he would think about on rainy days but never once dare *use*. He was too damn stubborn to run…*and admit it,* he told himself, crossing his sitting room to the chamber door, *you're too damn comfortable with this life to give it up just yet.*

When he opened his door, two pikes dropped into an X before him, trapping him inside. "Your Highness," one guard said, snapping to attention. "Please, stay inside."

"I shall not." Amery straightened his back to stand at his full height, just shy of six feet. "Remove your weapons, men. I am the regent."

But the pikes did not budge. "Sir Tovin's orders," the other guard bellowed. "The regent is to stay put."

A deep heat rose to color Amery's cheeks. "Stay *put!*" he spat. "I am not some recalcitrant child or…or…or a *prisoner* in my own kingdom! I will *not* be shuffled aside. I am—"

"In danger, Your Highness." With a clink of metal, the first guard tipped the visor on his helmet. "With all due respect, Sir Tovin requests that you remain here. We have increased your personal guard and have more men blocking the corridors that lead to your chambers. This really is the safest place to be."

Tovin's arms would be safer, Amery mused, but he kept those words to himself. With a final glower at both guards, the regent slammed his door shut, arms crossed as anger whirled through him. He wanted to be on the parapets, sword held high, leading his people to victory. His hair would whip out behind him like a banner, the crown gleaming atop his head—

The crown.

Out loud, Amery muttered, "I don't *want* the crown. I don't want to fight." He stormed across his chamber; at the fireplace, he turned on his heel and raged back to the door. His voice rose as he paced. "I don't want to *be here*, locked up in my own goddamn *room*, while Tovin is out *there*, in *danger.*"

With a furious cry, Amery overturned the dessert tray by his chaise lounge. Grapes and berries scattered before him, plates shattered on the stone floor, cakes smashed. He had stationed Tovin here to be with him, and he wasn't. To be *safe*, and he *wasn't.* If anything happened to him, anything at all, it would be Amery's own fault.

How would he ever live with himself then?

His mind turned back to the abandoned sluiceway. It wasn't an option; even if he wanted to run, Tovin had him trapped here, unable to leave. Because maybe...

A terrible thought occurred to him, rising like bile in the back of his throat. Maybe Tovin didn't *want* him to go. Maybe the knight was ready to sacrifice their love for the common good, just as he would give up his life to protect the regent's own.

No.

Amery flew at the door, beating it with his fists, kicking it, screaming obscenities at it that the guards on the other side must have blushed to hear. "No," he cried, like a spoiled kid throwing a tantrum. "No, I forbid it. Tovin!"

Once spoken aloud, his lover's name dispersed his anger; he slid to the floor, spent, struggling to hold back tears that choked and blinded him. "Tovin," he sighed. Bringing his knees up to his chin, he wrapped his arms around his legs and hugged himself into a tight ball, burying his head against his knees. *Please don't take him from me,* he prayed. *I shall give up my position here, this castle, this life, mine in exchange for his, please.*

There would be no more seesawing over the crown, no more question about where his loyalties lay. With his lover, with Tovin—nothing else mattered to Amery. As the castle rumbled around him, the sounds of battle rising thinly into the night, Amery vowed that if Tovin survived, then he would leave the castle behind.

Just bring him back to me, he prayed. *Let him live, and you can have your crown.* In his mind, it was a bargain struck with the gods above, his kingdom for his man. He only hoped they kept their end of the deal.

✦

THE REGENT LOST count of the minutes that passed. His legs grew numb, his buttocks sore, from sitting hunched before his chamber door. He felt dead inside, empty; it kept the fear at bay. His ears strained to follow the tides of the battle beyond the castle walls, but he could not distinguish the barbarian's victorious cries from those of his own men. The only thought that kept him from hysterics was the belief, however erroneous, that his heart would know if Tovin fell. Amery was sure of it. If his knight died, the color would drain from the world around him and his soul would weep. Until that happened, Tovin must still be alive.

Through the door behind him, he heard shouts and ringing footsteps, the clash of arms, a rallying battle cry. "For Pharr!"

Were the guards getting antsy, pinned down so far from the fight, that they had taken to sparring together to hone their skills? Perhaps Amery could sneak out now…or better yet, convince the guards to stand with him, follow him to the parapets—to Tovin's side.

Scrambling to his feet, he pushed the chaise lounge over to the fireplace, then leaped up onto it and reached for the sword and shield that hung above the mantle. His father's weaponry, already baptized in battle. The sword had a blunt, awkward blade, one Amery was uncomfortable using, but he needed something to protect himself…

Angry shouts from the corridor distracted him. He paused for a moment, listening to the scuffle beyond his door, but the sword grew heavy in his hands and he lowered it to the chaise lounge. For a few breathless moments he struggled with the clasp on the scabbard's belt, intending to wear it around his waist, but the buckle was old and the leather worn. He couldn't seem to get the clasp free.

"The hell with this," he muttered. Ignoring the clasp, he drew the sword and tossed the scabbard away. It would only hinder him. Setting the sword's tip against the furniture beneath his feet, he rested the flat of the blade against his leg to prop it up. Almost instantly, the sharp tip pierced the fabric of the chaise lounge, and sank a few inches into the mattress. White downy feathers escaped around it, as if Amery had speared a bird.

Turning back to the mantle, Amery tugged at his father's shield. It was bulky, fastened to the stone wall by a series of hooks and almost invisible wire that seemed impossible to unravel. He lifted the shield toward him, then ran a hand beneath it, feeling for the hooks he knew had to hold it in place. But the damn shield would not work free from its restraints. "Come on," he breathed. The polished metal warmed beneath his hands, fogging with his breath. Where he touched the shield, he left fingerprints streaked across its surface. "You *fucker.*"

Gods.

The heat from the fireplace brought a fine sweat to his brow, and he stared at his own fevered reflection as he tugged on the shield. *Bring Tovin back to me,* he prayed again. *That's all I'm asking for at this point. Let the barbarians have the castle if they must, just give me back my man.*

Selfish? Hell, yeah. But he's mine. Do you hear me? Mine.

He slipped his hands beneath the shield again, fingers strumming across the wires that held it in place, when he heard the door creak open behind him. In his chest, his heart somersaulted in relief. *Tovin…*

It wasn't him. In the shield's reflection, Amery saw a soldier enter his room. The regent froze, his breath caught in his chest, every muscle pulled as taut as a drum skin. The soldier's lack of armor told Amery this was not one of his guards; no chain mail protected his chest, no heavy plates covered his thighs. He wore what looked like rags—a loose fitting shirt negligently tucked into flowing breeches made from a dark animal hide. Dingy fur draped his shoulders, and he wore a boar's skull as a mask to hide his face. Hair like fire erupted over the top of the skull, a shade more orange than Amery's, and when he turned his back on the room to peer out into the corridor, the regent saw a braid hanging down the stranger's back that mirrored his own.

For a brief second the regent wondered if he were seeing things. In one hand, the stranger held a long, ragged blade, but the relaxed angle of the knife suggested he had not yet noticed Amery. He turned in a full circle, moving slowly, as if ensuring he had not been followed, then saw the carafe of wine on the credenza. He moved toward it, his back to the fireplace.

He did not know he was not alone.

Abandoning the shield, Amery pulled the sword from the chaise lounge and leveled it at the man's back. In a regal voice, he demanded, "Who are you?"

With a snarl, the stranger turned and raised his own blade. When he saw the regent, he lunged.

Amery jumped off the chaise lounge to meet the attack. His skills were rusty, but had he not watched the best knights in his land duel amongst themselves time and again? Mimicking Tovin's moves, hoping he looked even a fraction of the swordsman his lover was, Amery parried the stranger's blade aside. As the man stumbled past him, the regent brought his sword down on his exposed back, knocking him to the floor.

Is that it? He laughed, a wild sound that he strangled before it could get away from him. When the man didn't move, Amery dared to prod him with the tip of his shoe. *That was a bit easy*—

Without warning, the stranger lashed out, kicking Amery's legs from under him and bringing the regent down hard on the floor. King Adin's sword clattered out of Amery's hand as he fell, but before he even hit the ground, he was rolling away from the stranger. The jagged blade struck the stone floor inches from his face, hot sparks flashing between the metal and rock to blind him. He reached out for his sword, cut his fingers on the blade as he fumbled for the hilt, then felt the stranger's hot breath on the back of his neck as he tried to make it to his feet. The door, Amery thought. He just had to make it that far. Then maybe one of his guards could save him, or he could run.

Despite the hands clawing at his coverlet, Amery managed to stand. He used the sword for leverage, pulling away from the stranger before the twisted knife his attacker held could strike into the regent's back. Staggering away, Amery turned to face his opponent, and flinched at the skull-covered face that gleamed at him with malice. *Tovin, where are you now?*

Beneath the bony mask, the barbarian grinned, and Amery felt fear like sweat trickle down his back. With both hands on the hilt of his father's sword, he raised the blade between them, ready to fight.

CHAPTER 11

ON THE PARAPETS far above the regent's chambers, Tovin turned from the ledge in disgust. The castle guard were losing, and badly. Where were his own men? When would his friends' armies join them? Where the hell was Giles?

Questions he could not answer. He had sent another runner south, to spur his men faster. With any luck they would reach the castle by morning, but could the guard hold out against the barbarians that long?

Tovin didn't think so. Already renegade bands of the Cyrians entered the castle through the servants' quarters, where no one stood to fight. There was little he could do here, so far above the troops, except watch the battle and hope the tide would turn against their foes.

And what about Amery? Was he safe?

Turning to Berik, he snapped, "You're in command of the ramparts."

Berik watched Tovin storm toward the nearest stairwell. "Where are you going?" he called out.

"To find the regent." Tovin hoped the guards assigned to

Amery realized just how much they protected. With any luck, his lover was still in his chambers, still naked even, waiting for Tovin to show up. The longer it took the knight to return, the more pissed the regent would become. What did it matter if they were at war, if Amery's libido went unsatisfied?

The thought made Tovin smile. He took the steps two at a time, drawing his sword as he reached the corridor. The clash of arms rang through the stone, and when he rounded a corner he found Cyrians fighting his own men, hammering at them with their twisted blades and wooden cudgels. Fighting his way through the melee, Tovin hurried through the halls that led to the regent's chambers. *Please,* he prayed, hacking at anyone who came in his path, friend or foe alike. *Let him be safe.*

The door to the regent's chambers stood ajar. Tovin's throat closed to see it—he should have stationed himself here, at this door, and held the barbarians at bay himself. Where were the guards assigned to protect the regent? The corridor was empty save for a bloody handprint on the wall and an abandoned helmet that rolled over the stone when Tovin kicked it. Breaking into a run, Tovin crossed the length of the corridor and pushed through the door, his heart fluttering like a trapped bird in his chest. "Amery?" he called out.

Oh Gods.

In the center of the regent's sitting room lay a man on his stomach. Blood pooled around the obviously dead body, turning the dark clothing black. A long, red braid trailed down the dead man's back, the ends of the hair curling where they were dipped in the blood.

Tovin fell to his knees, tears stinging his eyes. *Too late. Oh Gods above, I was too damn late.*

Gently he reached out and placed a loving hand on the body's still warm back. His fingers brushed the plaited hair, which felt coarse and dry to the touch. Amery's hair had always been such a vibrant part of his being, so soft, so thick, so *alive...*

So beautiful. This wasn't Amery's hair.

With a frown, Tovin brushed the braid aside. The color was all wrong, the shade more garish than Amery's—how often had he seen it spread out against his own skin? It was much darker than this, much thicker, too, and when Tovin peered closely at the clothing on the body, he didn't recognize it. Beneath the braid was an animal's pelt, and the breeches were cut wrong. Ignoring the blood on his hands, Tovin rolled the dead man onto his back.

The man's face belonged to a stranger.

This isn't him. It's similar—the hair, yes, and maybe the body shape overall, but the facial structure is different. Those weren't the regent's lips—Tovin knew, he had kissed them often enough. He thumbed open one eye and stared at the muddy brown depths already beginning to fill with blood. Amery's eyes were a light green, almost translucent, like deeply cut crystal goblets filled with dry white wine.

This was not the regent.

He almost swooned with relief. Choking back his emotions, Tovin raised his voice into a hoarse cry. "Amery?"

"Here," came the reply.

The knight turned toward the doorway that separated the regent's rooms. There Amery staggered from the bedroom, his father's sword dragging across the stone floor. Tossing the blade aside, he took a shuddery breath and opened his mouth to say something more, but the look he threw Tovin was torturous. Those pale eyes were haunted—they had seen too much, knew too much, and for once, the regent could not speak.

Rising to his feet, Tovin caught his lover in a strong embrace. "Ye Gods," he sighed as he stroked Amery's back. His arms tightened around the regent at the thought that moments before he believed this man, *his* man, to be dead. He had not believed he would hold this body against his again, kiss this soft skin, hear the trembling draw of familiar breath in his ear. He hugged Amery tight, fisted his hand in the thick plait of hair that hung from his lover's nape, breathed in the scent of perfumed oil and sweat that, despite the circumstances, could still stir his groin. *Thank you.* "Amery, gods, I thought that was you."

With a shaky laugh, the regent whispered, "So did I."

He clung to Tovin, his whole body shaking like a tear poised to fall. Against Tovin's shoulder, Amery sobbed, "My decision is made. I swore if you came back to me, I would abdicate, and here you are. Here you are."

His fingers clenched Tovin's mail with faint, metallic clicks. Tovin wasn't sure what his lover meant, who he'd bartered with, but that did not matter—he was here, safe in Tovin's arms. Kissing the regent's ear, the knight murmured, "If you're serious about this…"

"I am," Amery whispered. "The sluiceway. Your sister's—"

"Go," Tovin told him. He kissed Amery's trembling lips and forced a smile. "I shall find you there, I promise."

But when he gave Amery a gentle shove toward the door, his lover shook his head. "Wait. Shouldn't I make a royal announcement or something? Tell them…" His face blanched, and his eyes searched Tovin, begging for reassurance. "You don't think they'll *make* me take it, do you? Hunt me down, or kill us both? Tovin—"

"Shh." The knight placed a finger over the regent's lips, silencing him. With a glance to indicate the fallen man at their feet, Tovin said, "They won't bother if they think you're dead."

"Wha—"

Slowly, so the regent would catch his drift without him having to say the words aloud, Tovin said, "I thought that man was you."

Amery's eyes widened in understanding. "You know me best," he murmured. "If it fooled you—"

"If no one looks too closely," Tovin added. "If he wore your clothes, and his face were burnt beyond recognition…"

"Yes," the regent sighed. His brow cleared, his shoulders sank as if a heavy weight had been lifted from them, and his smile flashed out clear and pure like the springtime sun. "Gods, yes."

When he didn't move, Tovin kissed him again and pushed him toward the door. "Now. Before you change your mind."

"I won't," Amery assured him. "I've never wanted anything so bad as I do you. Nothing I lose could compare to losing you."

"Then go."

The regent gave him one final kiss—a sweet press of lips that promised a lifetime more. His hands loosened in Tovin's armor and touched the exposed skin of his neck before cradling his face, holding him still as their mouths touched. His tongue darted into Tovin with a quick taste, as if he wanted just a little more. Tovin poured his heart into the kiss, relishing it, savoring it. He didn't know when he'd kiss his lover again.

Then Amery was gone.

✦

HOURS LATER, A rallying cry sounded outside the castle walls, and Tovin fought his way to the ramparts again. As he came to stand beside Berik, his old friend laughed and clapped him on the back. "He's alive!"

For a heart-stopping moment, Tovin thought the knight meant Amery. "Who?"

Berik pointed to the west, where a mass of men astride foaming steeds rode from the forest at a full gallop. The sight of Pharrisian troops rejuvenated the castle guards, and a shout rose from the parapets. "He must've found Giles," Berik yelled over the din. "Those yellow standards are his colors, and the orange belong to Lohden. His men are here, as well. The wily bastard, he's still alive, can you fucking *believe* it?"

Tovin forced a thin smile at his friend's laughter. In a soft voice, he admitted, "We may win this one yet."

By dawn, the castle was secure. Dark oil like blood streaked the exterior walls, the fuel still burning in some patches. The walls that had been pulled down or battered apart stood out in the bright sunlight like gaping battle scars waiting to be healed.

The moat around the castle ran thick with black blood; the fields, the forest, and the courtyards all held their share of dead or dying troops. Despite the castle's ragged appearance, most of the dead were Cyrians.

Shortly after sunrise, another battle cry sounded from the south. Like an injection of fresh blood, Tovin's own troops filled the already embattled armies with new hope. They battered back the enemy until only small pockets of resistance held out against the knights, and the majority of the Cyrian army lay slain or captured. When the head of the barbarian king rose from the carnage on a pike, brandished high for all the troops to see, Tovin knew the battle had been won.

Later, he strode through bloodied halls toward the regent's rooms, Berik by his side. His nerves felt like a stone in the pit of his stomach, and his face was a mask that hid his emotions. As his footsteps rang off the stone walls, he wondered if he had the strength to do what needed to be done. Amery was safe, he knew that, but he was the only one…

Kicking his way into the regent's chambers, Tovin frowned at the body on the floor. Face down once again, the stranger was now dressed in Amery's coverlet and tights, his own clothes long since burned in the fireplace. Though Tovin himself had dressed the man, his appearance still jarred him with a nasty shock. *Amery is fine*, he assured himself. *This is not him*. Still, he could not keep his hands from fisting at his sides, nor curb the rapid-fire stutter of his heart.

Berik pushed past Tovin to kneel by the body. "Gods," he sighed. "Your Highness…"

Tovin shut his eyes. He knew what Berik would see when he turned the body over—blood marred features Tovin himself had burned with the poker from the fireplace. The fire had singed off the bangs that Amery never had, had melted those muddy eyes so they would not give him away, and the barbarian's skull mask had been ground to fine dust beneath the heel of Tovin's boot. For all purposes, the body that lay in its pool of congealed blood *was* the regent. There was no way anyone would know otherwise.

Forcing a strangled sob, Tovin choked out, "Is he...?"

He knew he was. Of *course* he was. The knight had felt the cold muscles stiffen as he dressed the body in the regent's own clothing after Amery left.

But Berik did not know that. With a slow nod, he sighed. "He's dead."

Now Berik thinks he's gone, he thought, watching his friend struggle against tears. *And Lohden, and Giles...we were friends once, all of us.*

But he was mine first. And now he's mine, forever. He's free. I just have to get to him.

✦

TOVIN ANTICIPATED A scramble for the crown when the regent's death was announced. The castle advisers did not disappoint him. Before the body was even interred, Bellona had already organized a petition that called for a democratic vote among the landed gentry, weighted in her favor. Another adviser suddenly recalled a distant cousin of Amery's who might be next in line to the throne, and even a few of the guards polished off their credentials to parade before Mordrent. As the oldest adviser, Mordrent found himself in the unenviable position of viceroy until a king was crowned.

For two days, the castle was draped in black banners. The guards and knights wore black armbands as a sign of respect. The corridors were filled with the soft sound of servants weeping or speaking in hushed tones. Chambermaids gathered in small groups to gossip in whispers; whenever Tovin strode past them, they broke off and gave him such mournful sighs that he took to avoiding the women altogether. More than once he heard his name mentioned in passing, but when he turned to confront whoever had said it, no one met his stern gaze.

As castellan, Tovin stood at attention throughout the regent's funeral. *The regent* was how he thought of the body in the wooden casket; it helped ease the ache that had settled in his arms at Amery's absence. The service was short, and afterward the troops buried the regent with the soldiers who had fallen in battle. Throughout the day, Tovin stood watch over his men, the sun in his eyes, as they buried hundreds of nameless bodies, fellow warriors, friends.

By the time the last spadeful of dirt was tossed into the final grave, night had fallen. Tovin roused himself from his stone-like stance, surprised to find that torches had been lit to throw back the darkness. Despite the late hour, Tovin left the field and entered the castle, heading for the viceroy's chambers. He had to knock twice to rouse the slumbering Mordrent, who opened the door a crack and peered out at Tovin, not quite able to recognize the knight. "Yes?" he muttered. "You are…?"

"The castellan," Tovin replied. Then he ripped the black band from his arm, shucked off his mail, and dropped both to the floor. His sword followed suit when he unbuckled its scabbard from his waist. "I could not protect the regent—I am unfit to guard your castle."

The door widened, and Mordrent leaned out to glance down the corridor. His white hair was frazzled with sleep, like a dandelion gone to seed. "But…"

"I am sorry, sir." Untying the plates of armor that protected his legs, Tovin told the viceroy, "Goodbye."

Without further word, he turned, leaving the viceroy staring after him in disbelief.

CHAPTER 12

EARLY THE NEXT morning, Tovin sat astride his horse, the same steed he'd ridden into this courtyard not a week prior amid trumpeted fanfare. Now the sky was dank and gray, as if the clouds themselves wept at the regent's "death." Around him, his three friends had gathered—three strong men made weak with the loss of Amery. Part of Tovin wanted to tell them his lover lived, if only to relieve the ache he saw in those closed, hard faces, but there would be too much explaining to do, and word might leak out, putting himself and his lover in danger. Better that things should end this way, he believed. At least then there was some sense of closure.

Blinking back tears, Lohden patted the horse's neck and suggested, "You could stay."

"I cannot." Tovin held the reins tightly, causing the steed to prance in the courtyard. By the harsh light of day, the castle looked scarred and battered, but at least it still stood beneath the regent's flag. Tovin squinted into the sun and thought about the ride to his sister's inn. Two days, if he rode fast. He hoped Amery had made it.

Glancing around at his friends, he told them, "You don't understand."

Giles gave him a wry grin. "Ah Tove, we do. Probably more than you think."

"He was always special to you," Berik mumbled. His voice seemed to rumble deep within the bushy beard that obscured his face. "We always suspected there was something more to it than what you wanted us to see."

With a frown, Lohden turned to Berik. "Like what?"

The others laughed; the sound was thin and sparse in the early light, but it brought a ghost of a grin to Tovin's face none-theless. Leave it to Berik to guess at the brunt of their relation-ship. The man only thought with the head between his legs.

When their laughter tapered off, Giles told him, "Please don't leave thinking it was your fault. You did all you could—"

"It wasn't enough." Tovin laughed, a hollow sound in the quiet aftermath of the battle. "I was stationed here to guard *him*, remember? That was my sole charge. And I thought he wanted me to protect the damn *castle*."

He waved a hand around them, indicating the stones that still stood tall. "What use is it now, with him gone? It's hollow, a shell left behind on the beach, to be picked up and tossed aside. I should have protected *him*. The castle stood on its own, with little help from me. I failed."

Lohden started, "You didn't—"

But Tovin shook his head and interrupted his friend. "I thought I was the best, you know? I could beat any man with a sword—how many times did I out-fence each of you? But I couldn't even save him."

Berik blinked back tears and sighed. "You *are* the best," he told Tovin. "You're still alive. The viceroy needs someone like you, a commander in charge of his forces, and you're the only man for the job, you know it."

"I cannot do it," Tovin said again. With a spur of his heel, he turned his steed toward the open gate that led from the courtyard to the southland below. To Amery. He gave his friends one last glance over his shoulder, and forced a smile for their sake. "I am sorry."

Lohden raised a hand halfheartedly in farewell. Giles hugged himself tight as he watched Tovin ride away, and Berik pressed his hands to his eyes as if to keep tears from falling. Tovin knew he would not see them again, and the thought made his own eyes sting. Silently he prayed to whatever gods had looked after Amery to keep watch over his friends, as well.

Then he set the castle to his back and headed home.

✦

STACIA'S WAS A small inn on the outskirts of Konstas, a port city in the south of Pharr. Tovin's family came from the area, but he himself had grown up in the castle, training among the knights who served the king. Riding up to his sister's inn, he dismounted at the door and tossed the reins of his lathered horse to the stable boy who sat on the ground. He'd made the trip in record time, and his steed's heavy pants proved it. Digging out a gold denier from his saddlebag, he removed the bags from the pommel of his saddle and threw the coin at the boy's feet. The kid scrambled to attention. "Brush her down, boy."

Inside, a few men sat around weathered tables, and the barmaids who hurried around the floor glanced at Tovin as he stepped up to the counter. His sister tended the bar, her back to the room as she wiped down an empty mug. Without turning toward him, she called out, "What can I do you for, sir?"

"Stacia," Tovin said.

Recognizing his voice, she glanced over her shoulder, a smile already in place. Twin spots of blush colored her cheeks, lighting up her heart-shaped face. She had the same sandy blonde hair he did, the same stormy eyes, but her features were rounder, softened by years and the children she'd borne. "There you are," she cooed. "We were beginning to wonder…"

"I was delayed," Tovin explained. "Burying the dead, then being stripped of rank tends to do that to a man. Is he—"

"Upstairs," she replied. Concern flickered across her features. "In your room. He's terrified, Tovin. What happened?"

With the back of his hand, Tovin motioned around the main room and told her, "I'm sure you've heard. Gossip travels twice as fast as any steed." Pushing away from the counter, he headed for the wooden stairwell at the back of the room. "Is he all right?"

"He'll survive," she told him.

Tovin winked at her. "Thanks."

The inn's tavern and kitchens comprised the first floor; rented guest rooms filled out the second. The third floor was naught but a finished attic that had been divided into sleeping quarters for Stacia, her husband and children, and her staff. Tovin's room was a small space partitioned off the others, a place he stayed when not in the Konstas garrison or stationed at the castle. The door to the room was shut, and Tovin stopped before it, listening. The only sound he heard was raucous laughter from downstairs, but he sensed a presence on the other side of the closed door. It felt occupied, lived in, full. Like his heart. Cautiously, he eased the door open and stepped inside.

Amery lay curled on his bed, asleep. Tovin closed the door behind him and crept across the room. Since he had last seen his lover, Amery's long hair had been sheared, leaving a dark red fuzz over the top of his head. Stacia's doing, no doubt. Tovin reached out to run a hand along the buzzed cut—the short hair stood up beneath his palm and felt impossibly soft, like bristles on a baby's hairbrush. To keep him from being recognized. *Stacia, I love you.*

Beneath his touch, Amery let out a pitiful sigh.

Gently, Tovin lay down beside him on the bed. Taking his lover into his arms, he kissed Amery's lips tenderly, his fingers caressing smooth cheeks. Roused by his lover, Amery yawned, sleepy. "Tovin?" he murmured.

"Right here," Tovin replied. He kissed Amery again, his tongue parting those sweet lips to delve into his lover's mouth. Hunger rumbled through him at the kiss, and he found himself leaning Amery back to the bed, eager for more than this mere press of flesh. He wanted, *needed*, to feel this man around him once again.

Trailing kisses down Amery's neck, Tovin murmured into his skin, "It's over, love. Everything's over. It's just you and me, the way we always wanted it to be."

Amery smiled, and Tovin knew that they could live without the sword or the crown as long as they had each other.

ABOUT THE AUTHOR

J. M. SNYDER lives in Virginia. A graduate of George Mason University, Snyder is a multi-published, best-selling author of gay erotic and romantic fiction who has worked with several e-publishers, most notably Aspen Mountain Press, Amber Allure Press, eXcessica, and Torquere Press. Snyder's short stories have appeared online and in anthologies by Alyson Books, Cleis Press, and others.

In 2010, Snyder started JMS Books LLC to publish and promote her own writing as well as queer fiction, nonfiction, and poetry she enjoys.

Positive feedback as well as hate mail can be forwarded to the author at jms@jmsnyder.net.

Made in the USA
Coppell, TX
25 May 2022

78144938R00066